S   w   e   e   t

In some ways, there is n   ....to the joy of the human condition than music and sex. Music can be as soothing as a gentle kiss, or as powerful as an orgasm. The most powerful music can make your heart beat faster and make the hairs on the back of your neck rise in excitement and expectation. Music can make you move, moan, dance and shout. Music is to the soul as orgasm is to the body.

Music and sex are so visceral, so sensual that it seemed obvious to combine them. This book is that combination. Five talented authors have written five tales of sex and music, and the results are absolutely beautiful.

If, as you read, you find your fingers beginning to drift, your body starting to move, and a rhythm rising within you, do not be alarmed. Let Strummed take its toll until you too sing out loud!

-Kojo Black

Strummed

compiled by Kojo Black

S

SWEETMEATS PRESS

A Sweetmeats Book

First published in Great Britain by
Sweetmeats Press 2013

ISBN 978-1-909181-20-5

Printed and bound by CPI Group (UK) Ltd, Croydon, CR0 4YY.

Sweetmeats Press
27 Old Gloucester Street
London
WC1N 3XX
England, U. K.

Contents

For music lovers, and for musical lovers

Well Played

◆◆◆◆

by Stella Harris

Isabel tripped on her way into the audition hall. It was the exact opposite of the first impression she'd hoped to make, which is why it was probably inevitable. She's good, she knows she is, but she still has issues with her confidence when it comes to proving herself.

The people sitting in the front row turned to look at her, and when she found a certain set of piercing blue eyes assessing her she almost tripped again. *Damn.* She didn't know he'd be here, too. Kurt Christou, the first chair of the cello section — and hopefully her future boss — was the most intimidating man she'd ever laid eyes on.

Isabel had attended countless performances of the symphony trying to get a read on him. His style, his manner of playing…anything to get a hint as to what he was looking for. But the man was an enigma. His playing was as close to perfection as she'd ever heard but she couldn't tell what pieces of himself he was putting into the music. From what she could tell, he was simply a conduit for the will of the composer — as impossible as that seemed — and she just couldn't figure out what part of his music was really *him*.

Pulling herself together, Isabel made her way to the front of the room and onto the stage, all eyes on her. She had to calm herself — she couldn't let a little stumble, and a ridiculously gorgeous man, ruin her chances at the job of a lifetime.

So Isabel sat, taking the lone chair on the stage, pulled her cello out of its case, and closed her eyes for a moment to compose herself. As her breath settled and she found her inner calm, she began to play, eyes still closed, until she lost herself to the music and forgot her surroundings and her audience.

She hadn't even realised she'd reached the end of the piece until the sound of scattered applause broke her from her reverie and, startled, she opened her eyes. The first person she saw was Kurt. He wasn't clapping but there was a faint trace of a smile, the only one she'd ever seen on his face. She decided to count that as a win, packed away her cello, and made a more graceful exit than her entrance. Then, all she could do was wait.

Luckily for Isabel's sanity, she didn't have to wait long. Just two days later she got a call from the music director of the symphony offering her a position in the training program. It wasn't quite what she was expecting or hoping for, but it wasn't a 'No' so she eagerly accepted. The details and contract arrived by email moments later. She was to join rehearsals for a thirty-day probationary period before they made a final decision. The rationale had something to do with ensuring that she meshed with the other cellists in the section and — most importantly — with Kurt, the first chair.

She'd dreamt about meshing with Kurt more times

than she cared to count, but she didn't figure that was what they had in mind. Pulling her mind out of the gutter she updated her social media status — she'd been thinking about what to say all morning — and hurried to pack everything she'd need for the month. She felt like she was going to performing arts camp all over again — though hopefully with fewer pillow fights.

Isabel's first day started well. Right away she was introduced to Ellie, one of the other girls in the cello section. Isabel knew from the many concerts she'd attended that the whole cello section was made up of female musicians, which seemed a little odd. But she supposed gender didn't matter — everyone was equal in music.

Next to Kurt, Isabel had spent more time watching Ellie than anyone else in the symphony. She was beautiful — obviously — but the way that she seemed transported by what she played is what made watching her so irresistible.

Kurt led rehearsal that first day and doled out complements sparingly enough that they were worth their weight in gold. The other girls in the section seemed nice enough, but Isabel didn't spend much time getting to know them. She was there to improve her craft and make the cut, not to make friends.

Each musician had an assigned practice space far enough from the dorms that they didn't interrupt one other, or disturb someone who might be trying to sleep. Everyone kept to their own schedule, which suited Isabel just fine. She'd always liked to practice in the evenings, often far into the night, and she liked having the privacy to do so.

The biggest practice space in their bungalow belonged to Kurt, of course. He seemed to get the nicest versions of everything, which she figured was one of the perks of being section chair. Unlike her room which was outfitted only with a desk and chair, his room had a couch, a bookcase, and even a closet, in addition to a desk and chair that matched her own.

She knew all of this because her practice space was right next to his — and his room even had a little window. He once left the curtain open and she hadn't been able to resist taking a peek. She quickly found that wasn't the only thing she couldn't resist.

Kurt kept a practice schedule similar to her own and if she listened carefully, ear pressed to the wall, she could hear the music coming from the room. Not only could she hear it but she could *feel* it; the slight vibrations in the wall and the more intense vibrations in her own body. It wasn't the same as being in the room with him, but it was enough to make her tingle and ache.

During these eavesdropping sessions, Isabel's cheeks would flush and her nipples would pucker against the fabric of her blouse, her mouth falling open to accommodate her sudden need for more air. She'd allow her knees to give out, as they'd been longing to do, until she lay curled up on the floor, ear pressed to the wall as the music washed over her.

On those nights, back in her room, Kurt's playing was all Isabel could think about as she lay in bed. She longed to be able to pull those sounds from *her* own cello. But even more than that, she longed for Kurt to pull sounds from her. To play her body the way he played his instrument; finding the spots that made her sing, made her cry out. Then she'd drift off into a fitful sleep, full of desire that knew no release.

The combination of fitful sleep and the frivolous distractions she allowed to interrupt her practice began to take their toll. She knew she wasn't at her best during rehearsal and it frustrated her. Glances from the other girls were bad enough, but when Kurt scolded her for the first time it rattled her to the core. She needed to get her head back in the game and get her playing up to the same level as the other girls if she was going to keep her spot in the symphony.

She skipped dinner that night to go straight to her practice space, but once she was in the room, cello in hand, she couldn't bring herself to play. The music just wasn't in her. She needed to recapture the spark and there was only one way to do it. It was risky, she knew, but as she eyed the wall between her own space and Kurt's, Isabel knew what she had to do.

Nothing inspired her like hearing Kurt play — but watching him play was something different all together. She couldn't think of a way to describe it that didn't sound cliché, but when she watched him play she knew she was in the presence of greatness. She needed a dose of that now.

Isabel listened at the wall for a moment and didn't hear any signs of movement, so she slipped out of her own practice room and moved toward the next door. No one else was around, but she looked both ways just in case. The window to Kurt's room had the curtains pulled tight, but Isabel didn't see any light peeking through the cracks.

Holding her breath and steeling herself, Isabel placed one hand on the doorknob and knocked on the door. She didn't want to barge in, just in case Kurt was inside. There was no answer. Heart pounding, she turned the knob and the door clicked open. There was no reason to keep their practice spaces locked, as only their section had access to this bungalow.

Isabel opened the door only far enough to slip inside and didn't bother to turn on the light. She settled down behind the couch, her back to the wall, and waited for Kurt to arrive. Dinner would be over soon and she knew his patterns and habits as well as she knew her own.

Isabel grew nervous as she waited in the dark. Maybe she should have just asked to sit in on his practice? But then she would have had to admit that her own playing was off — and after that day's rehearsal she didn't need to give him any more evidence that she was off her game. Telling herself that she was making the right decision, Isabel settled in to wait.

She didn't have to wait long. As soon as her heart rate had returned to normal she heard the door open and the room flooded with light. Her pulse began to speed again. What if he caught her? What would he say? What would he think?

Isabel held as still as she could and tried to control her breathing. She hoped Kurt would start playing soon so that he'd be less likely to hear small noises in the room — right now he'd be able to hear a pin drop.

Isabel heard the sound of the chair creaking, the cello case opening, and moments later the first beautiful notes filled the room. He was playing one of her favorite pieces, Bach's Cello Suite no. 1 in G Major, and Isabel was transported immediately. The magic was returning and she felt it flowing into her body and spreading through her, as though she were being submerged in warm water.

Isabel forgot everything but the music. Forgot that she was crouching in someone else's practice space where she shouldn't be. Forgot that day's bad rehearsal. Forgot everything that was at stake for her that month.

Her whole world narrowed to the notes being played mere feet away from her and the familiar tingle began to spread through her body. She recognised the feeling now and she craved it. Already kneeling on the ground, she didn't have to worry about her knees going weak.

A high note made the hair on the back of her neck stand on end and she raised a hand to soothe the now over-sensitive skin. She let her hand linger there for a moment, enjoying her body's heightened response to the touch. She let her hand trail down her neck, her chest, and across her breasts. Her nipples hardened almost painfully and Isabel had to suppress a gasp by biting her lower lip.

Her hand kept moving, as if of its own volition, or perhaps guided by the music. Her fingers found the sensitive peeks of her breasts and brushed across them once, and then again. She fought to keep quiet, and her teeth bit down so hard on her lip she feared she'd draw blood. Isabel's breath was coming faster now but this wasn't enough. She didn't just need to hear the music. She needed to see him play.

Moving as slowly and quietly as she could, Isabel leant forward until she could just see around the end of the couch. From here she had a perfect view of Kurt as he played. His unruly blonde hair fell into his face as his head turned from side to side. His hands moved with his instrument as Isabel's own hands explored her body. She felt as if he and she had both been taken over by the same invisible force.

Right and wrong didn't exist anymore — all that mattered was the music and she had no choice but to give in. She stopped fighting the impulse and let her hand slide beneath her skirt, beneath her panties, and into her wet cunt.

It was too much; she released the moan that had been building in her throat since Kurt had started playing. The music stopped almost immediately. Isabel froze and her eyes shot up, but that's all she had time to do before Kurt was standing over her, bow still in hand.

The worst part was that he didn't look surprised or disappointed or angry. He looked like finding her here was inevitable. Like this had been bound to happen from the beginning and she'd had no choice in the matter.

She hadn't even moved her hand. As he looked down at her, she was kneeling at his feet with one hand still shoved into her panties. The realization caused heat to flood across her face and chest. Isabel was sure she was bright red. She'd never even allowed a lover to watch her touch herself, and the idea that someone she idolized was seeing her like this was the most mortifying thing she could imagine.

"Come here," Kurt said. His voice wasn't raised but the command was clear. Saying no was not an option. Isabel hurried to comply but did so awkwardly, there was no graceful way to get out of her current position and she knew if she withdrew her hand it would be incriminatingly wet. She couldn't decide if that was worse than what he was seeing now. But most of all, she didn't want to be told again. So she stood as quickly as she could, folded her hands behind her back, and closed the short distance between them.

Isabel couldn't bear to meet Kurt's eyes, so she looked down and studied the distance between their feet. The silence was deafening, as if the room itself mourned the loss of the music and blamed her.

Kurt didn't direct her further; he just grabbed her by the back of the neck like a naughty puppy and guided her around to the front of the couch. He positioned her so that she stood in front of the sofa, her calves pressing into the soft cushions. Kurt resumed his seat and took his cello in hand once more, but he didn't begin to play. Instead he had another command for Isabel.

"Strip."

Isabel thought she'd heard wrong, or that he was joking, but his expression was deadly serious. "Don't make me tell you again," he said. That spurned her into motion.

Her hands shook as she reached for the buttons on her blouse — Isabel couldn't remember ever having been more nervous — not even during her audition. Kurt's cool blue gaze stayed on her all the while, assessing her the way he did when she played. Isabel blushed under the scrutiny.

She gave up on elegance and settled for efficiency, removing the rest of her clothes as if she were alone at the end of the day, and not being watched by the object of her fantasies.

"Sit on the couch, lean back, and keep your knees at least two feet apart." Kurt's instructions were spoken in a clear and precise tone, the same way he led rehearsals. Isabel tried to find the head-space that would allow her to follow his commands unquestioned, but her embarrassment kept getting in the way.

She paused for too long and Kurt tapped the end of his bow against the floor — just as he did when he was displeased in rehearsal. The familiar gesture was just what Isabel needed to make her body obey. She assumed the position Kurt requested, with a last internal struggle to force herself to spread her legs. "Good," Kurt said, and his praise was as intoxicating as ever. "Now finish what you started," he said, and resumed playing.

Isabel's head was spinning. He couldn't possibly

mean that she should touch herself while he watched. She couldn't do it…there was no way.

After a few bars Kurt paused in his playing and turned the full force of his gaze on Isabel. He pursed his lips and Isabel knew she had only a brief moment before he would chastise her. That thought overrode the embarrassment she was feeling and she managed to trail her hand back up her inner thigh, all the way to her cunt.

When it was clear that she was doing as asked, Kurt began playing again. Even through her mortification, the music had an effect on her. She couldn't believe she was doing this. But the shame only made her wetter — her body was betraying her. Isabel's hand shook, but she didn't dare stop. Kurt's eyes flicked up, to check on her, several times a minute. The rest of the time, he too was lost in the music.

His playing sounded even more transcendent than usual, if that were possible. But perhaps that was because Isabel heard it through the haze of her pleasure. Without knowing it, this was exactly what she'd wanted since the first time she'd heard Kurt play. There, at that distance, it was as though the music made love to her. She watched Kurt's hands fly over his instrument and she could *feel* that touch on her own body.

Her legs shook and it became hard to keep them open. But every time they closed even a few inches, Kurt's brow furrowed or his lips drew tight, and Isabel remembered herself and spread her legs wide again. She'd never cum like that before — legs spread apart instead of pressed tightly together — but she could feel it building now. Her body was shaking and her breathing was shallow. Her fingers moved at a frantic pace, sliding across the swollen, hardened nub of her clit. She was sure she's leaving a wet spot on the couch, but she couldn't be bothered to care. She was, after all, only doing what he'd asked for.

The tempo of the music increased — it was the first time Isabel had heard Kurt's playing stray from the tempo markings on the page. As the piece reached its crescendo Isabel reached one of her own, clasping her free hand to her mouth to stifle her cries.

Kurt held still until the echo of the last note faded from the room and then he looked directly at Isabel. "Be here again tomorrow, ten pm." He began playing the next piece without waiting for an answer. He didn't need one, really. Isabel had shown she'd do whatever he asked.

The following days passed in a blur. Isabel was more distracted than ever and her playing suffered. The one thing that changed was that Kurt no longer called her out in practice. Instead, she'd learn of his displeasure each night when she came to his room.

The tasks he had for her would vary. Sometimes he'd want her to rosin his bow, or to polish his cello case. Other nights she'd have to arrange his sheet music or write the rehearsal schedule. The one thing that didn't change was that the moment she came through the door she was expected to strip. "When you're in my room, you're naked," he explained to her on the first day of her service.

It was liberating, in a way. There were no hems to fiddle with, no bra straps to pull up. She didn't have to worry if what she was wearing was flattering. She was stripped bare and on display — Kurt saw everything that she was.

Tonight, he saw that she was nervous. "Rehearsal today was appalling," Kurt's tone didn't give anything away. Was he angry with her? "But you know that already."

"Yes sir," Isabel answered, not meeting his gaze. He'd never told her not to look him in the eye, but it didn't matter. She couldn't bring herself to look at him when she was like this.

"So…what should I do with you tonight?" Isabel's mind flooded with possibilities, but she knew Kurt didn't really want her to answer. "I need to listen to the recording of today's rehearsal and take notes. Not a pleasant task, to be sure. Maybe you can make it a little more bearable for me?" As he spoke, Kurt raised his hand, gesturing for Isabel to come forward. She did as he indicated, stepping into the space made between his open legs.

Kurt pointed at the floor and Isabel knelt before him. Even though she knew what had to be coming next, she was shocked to see Kurt pull off his belt and undo his pants. This was further than they'd gone before and Isabel's cheeks heated at the thought of what she was about to see.

She wasn't disappointed; Kurt's cock was as spectacular as the rest of him. Isabel's mouth watered and she began to lean forward, her rising lust betraying her modesty. A hand on her shoulder stopped her. "I take it you know what to do. Be sure to watch your teeth." Isabel bristled at the instruction. She might not have been as experienced as some, but she knew her way around a blowjob.

She leant forward again and this time he didn't stop her. She paused for a moment, just letting her lips brush against the head of his cock to savor the moment, but a hand on the back of her head cut the moment short. He pressed her forward and she had to open her mouth quickly to accommodate the pressure.

The recording of that day's rehearsal began to play and Isabel began to lose herself in her task, her thoughts drifting with the music. But then the first error became apparent.

Thwack. "You came in late there," Kurt said, and Isabel almost didn't hear him, she was so shocked that he'd hit her. "Don't stop," he instructed, thrusting his hips forward and almost choking her. Isabel began bobbing her head up and down again, not wanting to find out what would happen if she displeased Kurt further.

She tried to look to the side, to see what he'd hit her with, and just barely managed to see the belt he'd pulled off doubled in one hand. Seeing it frightened her, but upon reflection the strike hadn't really hurt so much as it had surprised her. Even Kurt couldn't be so crazy as to really hurt her when she was in a perfect position to hurt him back — badly. Perhaps that's why he'd given the warning about her teeth. She wasn't able to relax long before the next error played loud and clear.

Thwack. He did it again. "Sloppy articulation." He wasn't wrong but it still galled her to be told. She wanted to shout at him that her errors had been his fault. That she was off her game *because of him*, but somehow she knew he wouldn't be receptive to that argument. In a strange way she found the punishment freeing. As if by enduring it she was being absolved for her poor performance.

Kurt was incredibly hard in her mouth. Her jaw was getting tired from accommodating his girth, but she was also enjoying herself. She'd always enjoyed giving pleasure and she found a special satisfaction in making Kurt feel good. On the one hand she felt like he didn't really deserve this pleasure from her, but on the other it was one small way she had power over him. *She* was the one making him feel like this, *she* was the one who was going to make him cum. Even if for only a moment, he *needed* her.

Thwack. "Your dynamics are all over the place." This time she groaned. He wasn't hitting her very hard, but she was getting sensitive and each impact hurt worse than the one before. Kurt's cock throbbed when he hit her. He was getting off on this. She could feel the blood pulsing through his veins and she knew he was close.

Isabel slowed her pace to feel one more moment of control before it would all be over. But he couldn't even let her have that. Kurt's hand returned to the back of her head, his fingers threading through her hair and tightening, guiding her movements. She knew there was one more mistake coming from the rehearsal — a big one. She wondered if Kurt would miss it in his distracted state. She should have known better.

Thwack. "You missed the coda." His words were strained and before he'd finished speaking he was flooding her mouth, cumming so hard she almost choked on it. She would have pulled off if his hand hadn't held her tight. She squeezed her eyes shut against the tears threatening to spill out.

When he finally removed his hand, she pulled off quickly, gasping for air. "At least you do something well," he said, and the comment stung more than the belt. Kurt stopped the recording and adjusted his pants. He didn't need to tell her that she was dismissed, it was clear from his actions. Isabel dressed as quickly as she could and hurried out of the room. She'd left feeling bad about herself on other occasions, but this was a new low. Something had to change.

The quality of Isabel's playing continued to worsen, and with it her mood. She couldn't stop thinking about her last encounter with Kurt. She knew she had to break out of this cycle — what she didn't know was *how*.

She had to regain Kurt's respect, and there was only one thing that really mattered to him — the music. Isabel vowed to throw herself into practice before it was too late.

The next day, rather than keeping to herself as she

usually did, Isabel went down to the common room where she knew the other girls from the section met.

Freya, Ellie, Leah, and Grace were sitting around the card table laughing about something, but they went silent as soon as they noticed her. Isabel almost lost her nerve and left the room, but she knew she had to do this. She smiled, steeled herself, and stepped forward. It only took the other girls a moment before the smiles returned to their faces and Ellie hopped up from her seat to pull up an additional chair.

Isabel released the breath she'd been holding and gratefully took the seat that was offered. As if Ellie could read Isabel's mind and knew she didn't want a fuss made about her presence, Ellie resumed the conversation without drawing attention to Isabel's arrival. It didn't take long for Isabel to catch the thread of conversation; the girls were talking about ways to make black concert dress a bit more personalized. Perfect. This was exactly the kind of superficial banter she needed.

As soon as there was a break in conversation Isabel interjected with her thoughts about sequins. This started a lively debate about whether sparkling on stage was a fair way to assert your individuality or a completely rude distraction to your fellow musicians. Ellie took Isabel's pro-sparkle stance and they were joined by Grace. Freya and Leah were both anti-sparkle and a lively debate ensued. Before long they were shouting and laughing as though they'd been friends for the whole two weeks Isabel had been there — no apparent hard feelings remaining for her earlier standoffishness.

◆◆◆◆

Things got better as Isabel spent more time with the other girls. She changed her schedule so that she practiced during the day, and ate with the other girls in the dining hall at night. In the evenings she'd join them in the common room. Sometimes they'd get some additional practice in, but mostly they'd just talk and Isabel found that she really liked getting to know them. Best of all, Kurt would never come and interrupt the whole group to summon her to his room. Isabel's nightly visits stopped and, while he sometimes gave her looks that were easy to interpret, he never actually said anything.

Isabel feared that he was only going easy on her now because he planned to get back at her later. It could be as simple as saying she wasn't a good fit for the section when her probation period was over. Isabel just had to hope that ultimately the music would be more important to him than his own ego. It would be a close call for sure.

When Isabel got to the common room that night she found the other girls more dressed up than usual. She panicked for a moment, thinking she'd missed an announcement about a performance, but their outfits were all wrong for that.

"Isabel's here, it's time to go!" Grace announced, jumping out of her seat.

"Go where?" Isabel asked, confused. Now she knew for sure that she was missing something.

"Tonight we go out," Ellie answered, coming up to

Isabel and throwing an arm around her shoulders.

"Out?" Isabel asked, confused. She'd spent three weeks here and never once left the compound. Everything they needed was here, their food was provided for them, that was the whole point.

"Yes, out. It's time we all blow off a little steam, don't you think?" Ellie looked very excited about the idea as she spoke and Isabel already knew she'd lose if she put up a fight. Ellie didn't put her foot down often, but when she did, she won. Isabel had actually been thinking of getting in an extra hour of practice and then calling it an early night, but she could see she was outnumbered.

"I'll get my coat," Isabel said.

"That's my girl!" Ellie answered with enough enthusiasm that Isabel wondered if she'd already started drinking.

Isabel started to relax as soon as they were out. The girls had been right — Isabel hadn't realised how badly she'd needed a break. But now that she was out — away from the compound for the first time since she'd arrived three weeks before — it was clear that she'd needed this.

"Come on, it's about time you loosened up a little," Ellie said, putting a third cocktail in Isabel's hand. With her last sober thought, Isabel worried about having a hangover during rehearsal the next day but Ellie's brilliant smile persuaded her. Isabel could follow that smile into all kinds of trouble.

She took a sip, and then another, and the last of her worries melted away. She was laughing, the other girls were laughing, and everyone was swaying to the music. Every now and then one of the girls bumped into her and they all burst into laughter.

"So," Freya started, "you were spending a lot of time with Kurt." There was some bite to her words, but it was softened by the fog of alcohol. Leah shot Freya a look, and the other two girls grimaced, but no one tried to change the subject. They clearly wanted to hear what she had to say.

"Yeah," she offered, lamely. The four inquisitive looks aimed at her were clearly not satisfied. Her impulse was to run away, to hide her secrets like she usually did, but the cocktails had done their work and she was feeling reckless. "I showed up in his rehearsal space every night, stripped, and then did whatever he told me to," Isabel said in a rush, before she could lose her nerve.

A few eyebrows went up in response to her confession, but it wasn't nearly the reaction she expected. They were looking at her like there should be more to the story, like she hadn't gotten to the punch line yet. "Sometimes he made me touch myself while he watched," Isabel stuttered out, waiting for a big reaction, but none came. "And sometimes he made me go down on him while he listened to the playback of the rehearsal." The shock wasn't coming, the girls just looked bored now.

"He had Grace cooking for him and bringing him

dinner every night so he wouldn't have to stoop to the dining hall with the rest of us," Ellie announced. Grace swatted Ellie in the arm almost before she'd finished speaking. "Hey! Watch the drink!" Ellie shrieked when a few drops escaped from her glass and hit her shoe.

"At least I didn't take it in the ass," Grace retorted, glaring at Ellie.

"Hey!" Ellie shrieked again. They were starting to draw attention from the other bar-goers. Isabel was the one who was shocked now. She had felt so used, so ashamed, and her experience wasn't even unique.

Leah and Freya had matching constipated looks on their faces, perhaps worried that their own follies would be revealed next.

"So what you're telling me is that he does this to everyone? This is nothing new?" Yeah, Isabel was being a little slow, but she *had* been drinking.

"Yup. Every new girl goes through some kind of hazing. It's always different but it's always the same. Eventually he gets bored, or another new girl shows up, but nothing changes." Ellie gulped the last of her drink as she finished talking.

"Can't something be done about it? We could go to the musical director…something." The girls all looked at Isabel like this had never occurred to them. "He should have to pay for this, shouldn't he?" Isabel began to see the faces around her light up — she was getting through to them. "If we came forward together, they couldn't accuse us *all* of lying." The girls were listening, considering even, but Isabel could tell she hadn't won them over yet.

"That's a career killer, don't you think? Even if we do come forward together, who's going to want to hire a musician who went up against their section leader? There are so many people competing for every position, we'd never be able to prove bias if someone decided not to hire us." Leah said, and Isabel was afraid she had a point. But she was also still high on the idea of making this stop, making Kurt pay for what he'd done.

"I don't think it has to come to that. There's no way the symphony wants a scandal like this to come to light, they'd probably be willing to keep things quiet — handle the issue internally." Isabel could tell she was starting to lose her audience, but she wasn't ready to give up yet.

"What if we don't go to the music director?" Four faces perked up. "What if we just threaten to…. We go to Kurt directly and handle this our own way?" Isabel had them back; all the girls were focused on her and what she'd say next.

The plan formed as she spoke. Isabel didn't even know what was going to come out of her mouth until she heard the words herself. Four sets of eyes widened as the girls listened, and they got closer to Isabel to hear every word. Isabel felt powerful for the first time she could remember. Not only were these girls looking up to her, listening to her and willing to follow her plan, but she was going to stand up for herself, get revenge for being wronged for the first time.

She began to feel a warm glow inside that had nothing to do with the cocktails she'd been drinking.

The girls spent a few late nights working out the details of their plan. Isabel walked around so excited she was practically vibrating. Her playing improved and she was making friends she knew she'd have for life, no matter what happened with Kurt or with the symphony.

Freya drew the short straw and the girls sent her to tell Kurt they would be rehearsing in the smaller practice space that night. It was just as well that the task fell to her, she'd been around the longest and he had the least reason to suspect she was up to something. This part of the plan was vital because they couldn't be assured of privacy on the larger stage.

Isabel paced around her room several times, checking her reflection in the mirror each time, before finally going to meet the other girls in the common room. They'd agreed to meet there and walk to the practice space together in case anyone was losing their nerve or had any last minute questions.

Isabel entered the room and all eyes turned to her. Happily, all the other girls looked excited, rather than scared. As long as they stuck together, they'd be fine. Cello cases in tow, they made their way to the designated practice space for that night. They timed it so they'd be set up before Kurt arrived, but there was always the chance that he'd be early.

They filed into the room one at a time, Isabel at the back of the group. Everyone went to their usual seat and Isabel saw that the open seat for Kurt was exactly where they left it that afternoon. They each began to fill time in their own way — they didn't want Kurt to be suspicious when he showed up. Isabel tried to focus on tuning her instrument but her mind was too scattered. So she just played a few notes and hoped she looked sufficiently busy.

There was a noise at the door and Kurt entered the room. Isabel's heart rate immediately increased and she could feel the tension rise around her. She was sure Kurt noticed — he noticed everything — but he didn't comment. He set his cello case in the corner of the room and brought up his chair to face them. Kurt took his typical rehearsal pose: sitting back in the chair, legs crossed, one hand on his knee and one on his chin.

Admittedly, he looked as handsome as ever, blonde hair falling into his face, slim fingers near his mouth, long limbs folded up around him. Isabel almost lost her nerve; wondering how to signal to the other girls that the plan was canceled. But then Kurt saw her looking at him and he smirked, just one corner of his mouth lifting, and all her resolve returned. He felt just as superior as he always had, and it was time to do something about it.

Kurt waved his hand — the signal that they should begin playing — and the girls did so, as if tonight were the same as any other rehearsal. They'd all agreed that this part was important. They wanted Kurt to see how much their playing had improved, that they take the music as seriously as he does.

When the concerto came to a close Kurt opened his mouth to speak. He was about to critique their playing, but Isabel didn't give him the chance to get in a single word. "Actually, you're going to listen to us now," she said. At first she didn't feel the confidence her words implied, but the shocked look on his face gave her strength. "The thing is, Kurt, we've been talking." Isabel paused just long enough to enjoy the nervous look on his face. "We've decided that it's high time things change around here." Isabel was finding her groove; feeling powerful.

"I don't know what you think you're doing here Isabel, but your chance at a spot in this symphony is rapidly vanishing." Kurt stood as he spoke, and began to pace the room. Isabel could tell that he was nervous, but he wasn't going to just give in.

"See, that's where you're wrong," Ellie chimed in. Kurt turned to look at Ellie, and Isabel thought he may have just realised that they're all going up against him together. "We're tired of your threats. We're here because we're the best of the best — not because we jump through hoops for you," Ellie continued. It seemed like she was finding her own groove. Isabel couldn't take her eyes off Kurt and his reactions but, out of the corner of her eye, she saw that the other girls were relaxing too, as it became clear that they had the upper hand.

"We've decided that things are going to change!"

Grace almost shouted, so pleased to be speaking up, she was like a kid in a school play finally getting to her one line. Her interjection was jarring enough for Kurt's expression to shift. Isabel thought they might be losing him and she took control of the situation again.

"Here's the deal. We finally got around to comparing notes and we know you've been treating the cello section like your personal harem. We're not going to put up with it one minute more. Here's how it's going to go: you're going to keep your dick in your pants and treat us like professionals, and in exchange we're going to keep what's been going on to ourselves, rather than make a formal complaint to the music director." Isabel took a deep breath when she'd finished talking. All she could do now was wait for his reaction.

Isabel watched as varied expressions passed over Kurt's face. All the girls were looking at him, wondering what he'd say. Would he call their bluff, knowing they don't really want to make a public fuss? He opened and closed his mouth a few times; starting to look like a fish that wasn't getting enough air by the time he finally spoke.

"Okay," he said, and then there was a long pause. Isabel held her breath while she waited for what he'd say next. "You win." He had a way of saying the words that made it seem like he was still in charge. He'd agreed to their demands and yet somehow still looked smug. It was remarkable.

Isabel turned to look at Ellie and found the corners of her mouth turned down. Out of all the reactions they'd considered, this wasn't one of them. They'd prepared for rage, for refusal, even for tears, but not for calm acquiescence. Kurt stood there, looking at them, as though wondering what else they'd got. And, infuriating as it was, Isabel didn't know what to do about it.

"That's not all," Ellie said, and all eyes snapped to her. Isabel couldn't imagine what she had in mind, but she recognised the glint in Ellie's eyes and knew that it meant trouble. The other girls must have known it too, because they each had matching looks of concern on their faces. Kurt crossed his arms, as if challenging her to impress him.

"Get your cello," Ellie instructed, and all the girls shifted their rapt attention from Ellie to Kurt, wondering how he'd respond to a direct order. He took a moment, clearly unwilling to jump in response to a command, but he didn't wait long before crossing the room and fetching his instrument. He returned to the center of the room with it, looked back at Ellie, and raised one eyebrow.

Isabel's heart nearly burst through her chest. She had no idea where Ellie was going with this and she feared that it could blow the whole plan if Ellie tried to push Kurt too far.

"We've been your playthings long enough. Now it's time *you* played for *us*," Ellie said, not taking her eyes of Kurt. He took another moment, but eventually he sat in the chair and prepared to play.

"Any requests?" Kurt asked, still sounding smug. Isabel hoped Ellie knew what she was doing.

"Just play," Ellie told him and, with a shrug, he obeyed. It was a revelation. Isabel couldn't believe he was letting himself be pushed this far. But she still didn't know what Ellie's plan was. Isabel conveyed her confusion with a pointed look in Ellie's direction.

"He likes to watch, right? So lets let him watch. Only this time he doesn't have it his way. He doesn't' get to tell us what to do. He cannot touch. And he doesn't get to join in when he feels like it." Ellie's words didn't make any sense to Isabel at first, but Leah and Freya smiled as if they understand perfectly and they went to each other right away. Isabel's eyes widened as she watched the girls kiss. She'd thought they were friends, but she'd had no idea there was something going on between the two of them.

Ellie moved behind Kurt, rested her hands on the back of his chair, and leant toward his ear. She was close enough to him to whisper, but she spoke loud enough for the other girls to hear.

"All you get to do is play and watch. You don't stop playing until we tell you to. Understand?" Ellie asked, and Isabel feared she'd overplayed her hand. It took a moment for Kurt's expression to register understanding. To his credit, his playing never faltered. He gave a short nod and Ellie moved away from him to stand beside Grace.

"You're not the only one with a strong reaction to his playing," Ellie said to Isabel as she pulled Grace's cardigan off her shoulders. "Haven't you wanted to get off to his music?"

Isabel's face flushed as Ellie's words reminded her of the first night in Kurt's practice room. She'd told the girls about what he'd made her do, but she'd been vague about what she was doing in his room in the first place. Perhaps that wouldn't have been a surprise to them either.

"Of course you have…we all have," Ellie continued, not waiting for Isabel to answer. Ellie continued to undress Grace as she spoke, and Grace simply moved her body to make the task easier, raising her arms when required, or lifting a leg. Ellie and Grace looked as comfortable together as Freya and Leah, and Isabel began to understand that she'd been the odd girl out in more than one way.

"Lets show him exactly what he can't have anymore," Ellie said, sliding Grace's panties down her legs, leaving her standing in the room completely nude. But Grace didn't seem at all concerned. She didn't even look at Kurt, or the other girls — her eyes stayed glued to Ellie. Isabel looked at Grace's body; her smooth skin covered in goose bumps from tip to toe, her nipples peaked and hard.

Beneath her clothes, Isabel realised she was in precisely the same condition. She'd actually been distracted enough by what was going on around her that, for a moment, she hadn't noticed she was having the same reaction to Kurt's music that she always did. Her body was tingling in all the right places and her skin felt so sensitive that she was acutely aware of every inch of fabric on her dress.

"Join us," Grace said, holding a hand out toward Isabel.

Isabel hesitated. It wasn't as if she hadn't thought about it. Grace was beautiful, all the girls were, but she had to work with them — hopefully for a long time — and she didn't want to introduce any complications.

Ellie was undressed now too. She stood behind Grace and her hands came around Grace's body, stroking her stomach and making their way up to Grace's full breasts. Once there, she pinched Grace's nipples, making Grace sigh and arch her back as she rose up onto her tiptoes. Grace's own hand was still extended, and Isabel couldn't ignore the invitation any longer.

Isabel stepped forward and took Grace's hand. The next few moments ran together. Isabel was aware of hands on her body. Someone was stroking her hair and she felt the zipper of her dress coming undone. Before she knew it, she was standing on stage in only her bra and panties. But after what Kurt had put her through, it would take more than that to embarrass her.

In fact she rather enjoyed showing Kurt what he couldn't have any more. It was one thing to strip at his command. It was quite another to tease him with her body when there was nothing he could do about it.

Grace's hands cupped Isabel's face and their lips met in a kiss. Grace's lips were just as soft as they'd looked and Isabel lost herself in the sensation. She closed her eyes, let the music fill her head, and tried to give as good as she got; licking and sucking at Grace's lips. All the while Ellie kept working, and moments later Isabel was divested of her bra and panties. The three girls stood completely naked and it felt totally natural.

Isabel turned to see what Freya and Leah were doing and found them in a similar state of undress. They had moved to the couch on the side of the room and appeared to be completely focused on each other. Isabel didn't want to stare, but it was hard not to look at the way they were touching each other.

It was clear that they knew each other's bodies well. They moved with confidence, drawing responses from one another with every touch. Isabel could also see Kurt turning his head their way every so often. She was glad to see it was possible to distract him from his music — even if his playing didn't suffer for it. Kurt's eyes met Isabel's as she watched him and she resisted the urge to turn away. There was no reason for her to avert her eyes anymore. They were equals now.

Four hands slid across Isabel's body and her eyes fluttered — she had to struggle to keep them open but she wasn't willing to drop Kurt's gaze just yet. She saw a slight sheen of sweat on his forehead, a hint of pink on his cheeks, and she could imagine the bulge in his pants straining behind the wood of his instrument. Isabel felt intoxicated by the power of her sexuality. She wanted Kurt to see exactly what it looked like when she really abandoned herself to pleasure.

She let Ellie and Grace pull her down to her knees on the soft rug that stretched across the middle of the room. Even the simple touch of the soft strands against her legs made her tingle, she was already so sensitive.

Grace stroked her hair, pushed it out of her face, and

kissed her again. At the same time, Ellie pressed up against her back and Isabel could feel the swell of Ellie's breasts. She could even feel a slight tickle where the soft hair between Ellie's legs brushed against her ass.

With the music filling the room, the sounds Freya and Leah made just a few feet away, and the hands and bodies touching her, Isabel felt like she was high — floating on a cloud of sensation. She didn't even know what she should focus on. One moment she was listening to the music, letting it wash over her. The next she'd hear a gasp or some other noise from the girls on the couch and her attention would be pulled towards them. Then a hand would touch her neck, her breast, or her thigh and all she could focus on was skin against skin.

It was almost too much and it was wonderful. All of the stress, the worry, the anxiety she'd been holding in her body began to drain away. She listened to Kurt's playing and let all the passion she felt for the music fill her up. But rather than be overwhelmed by it, as so often happened when she was alone, now she had an outlet.

She pressed forward until Grace was forced to lay back. Isabel slid down on top of her and spent a moment just enjoying the way their bodies fit together. Grace opened her legs to make room for Isabel's body and Isabel gladly filled in the space. Grace's arms wrapped around her and Isabel savored how warm and soft Grace's embrace was. But she wanted more than Grace's embrace.

Isabel slithered down Grace's body until she could

bury her face between the other girl's legs. At the first touch of Isabel's breath, Grace sighed and her legs fell open. Isabel smiled to herself and went to work, first teasing with just the tip of her tongue; soft licks that made Grace's body jump in response.

Grace was so responsive it was a pleasure to play with her. Everything Isabel did elicited a reaction. Every touch, lick, scrape of teeth, had Grace writhing beneath her. Under any circumstances, this would have been incredibly gratifying. But now, knowing that Kurt was watching, it was even better.

Isabel didn't know the full story of what Kurt had done with Grace, but she was sure he'd never seen her enjoy herself like this before. Giving pleasure just wasn't what he did. Even his music, which should have been for the enjoyment of others, was another extension of his ego. Isabel saw that now, for the first time, and Kurt began to lose his appeal. His playing didn't make him great. It was just something he hid behind. The notes he played were still beautiful, but the man making them had lost his power over Isabel. The music was beautiful for its own sake — not because Kurt was the one playing it.

While Isabel's ministrations made Grace's back arch and her body tense, Ellie moved closer behind Isabel and steadied her hip with one hand. Isabel barely had a moment to wonder what would come next before Ellie plunged two fingers inside of her.

Isabel arched her own back and tried to focus on

what she was doing. Grace was close — she could feel it. Just a few more swirls of her tongue and Grace was crying out. She almost pushed Isabel away with the force of her body's undulations, but Isabel didn't stop licking until Grace's hands finally came down and grabbed her by the face, pulling her up for a kiss.

Now that she didn't have to focus on Grace's pleasure, Isabel was free to focus on her own. Ellie's hand was working her expertly and Isabel was surprised how quickly her body was responding. It usually took Isabel a while to guide someone and show them how to touch her in just the right way, but Ellie seemed to know by instinct what to do.

Isabel braced herself with both hands on the rug so she wouldn't crush Grace beneath her; and Grace's hands stayed on her face, steadying her and keeping their eyes locked. Isabel had to struggle to keep her eyes open. Grace was watching her so sweetly, so intently, Isabel didn't want to shut her out.

Ellie did something with her fingers that Isabel couldn't even define but it had an immediate effect. Her legs shook and the impulse to stretch out flat was hard to resist. But she wanted to stay where she was, to share this with Grace. Only a moment more and she was cumming, her eyes wide open and staring at Grace whose own expression mirrored Isabel's. As though the wonder of her pleasure were contagious.

Isabel barely had a moment to catch her breath before the bodies around her were reconfiguring. She was surprised to see that Freya and Leah had come to join them on the rug while she'd been distracted. Their limbs began to tangle with her own, with Ellie and Grace too, and it was clear that Isabel wasn't going to get to catch her breath for a while.

Isabel let go, allowed herself to sink into her surroundings; a symphony of bodies; moans, gasps, giggles, and squeals. All to the accompaniment of Kurt's playing. Isabel thought she'd found her deepest pleasure through music before, but she'd been wrong. This, right here, was as good as it got.

On Highway 17

◆◆◆◆

by B.Z.R. Vukovina

It may not have been Plymouth's prettiest '56 Savoy — pale woodland green with a russet, rusted underbody climbing past two parallel white-stripe highlights, all over dented and dinged — but its bald tires rolled sufficiently along the fresh asphalt of Highway 17 even as the battered engine wheezed and rattled. Breathing deeply in, Cob Augo didn't mind any of it because the road was winding and smooth, his guitar sat safely on the seat beside him and, through his driver's side window rolled fully down, the rushing air felt like noise against his ears, felt like time itself rushing by, sounding like fate and smelling of unspoiled dew mixed with the lacustrine aroma of the clear, calm, reflective surface of Lake Superior to the left meeting the fingertips-becoming-gnarly-mountainous-knuckles of the indestructible Canadian Shield to the right.

Ever since Sault Ste. Marie, where he'd bid goodbye to Lake Huron and most everything else, the road had been so empty that every sign of civilisation, whether town or Town & Country, was a well-intentioned slap to the face, a reminder that he had to keep conscious because, even here, he still wasn't alone in the world. Focus — he had to keep his.

A logging truck rumbled by in the opposite direction.

Cob gripped the steering wheel, and he checked the fuel gauge:

One-third left.

The truck disappeared into the rear view.

The Savoy's engine puffed, its body trembled and lurched.

Cob bounced.

The guitar strings resonated.

The engine was getting worse, its behaviour increasingly and violently erratic. Where had he first noticed it? Somewhere in New York State before the Canadian border. But it had been subtle then, just an irregular heartbeat. Now it was obvious. Now, it was getting dangerous. Maybe he'd stop and have the car checked after all. He could afford the time. He had it all worked out, and with a day to spare. Even going the long way, going the northern route, he had a day to spare.

The highway rose and ribboned around a rocky bluff.

Below, the lake was dispersing the day's sharp first light and for a moment Cob felt like he was driving straight into the brilliant water, destined to drown — or ignite — before the highway twisted away, down, and the lake was at his left again.

The road levelled off.

Cob took his palms from the steering wheel and rubbed them into his eyes.

He needed a break. He'd been driving too long.

So, that was the plan: if the next town he passed had a garage, he'd stop; he'd pay someone to listen to the engine while he drank a cup of strong coffee and maybe ate breakfast, maybe scrambled eggs and bacon.

His stomach grumbled.

He gripped the steering wheel. There wasn't a truck this time, just a realisation: 1,300 miles and the courage to take the first step were already behind him. Only 2,200 remained. One-third in the fuel tank, two-thirds left to travel, and then all would be good. He couldn't explain — or even understand — how he knew that, but he did. It was a certainty. Just get to Berkeley on time. Just do that and everything else will fall into place. *This is the challenge. This is the most important journey of my life.*

He glanced at the guitar.

It shone beautifully.

The town was called Black Bear Portage. The morning was windless and warm. The ruddy-skinned mechanic brought the hood of the Plymouth down with a gentle click and wiped across his forehead with a thick, oil-stained forearm. "Good car," he spat. "Bad engine."

Cob didn't say anything. He only felt indescribably thin in his thin trousers and the thin stripes of his shirt, his thin laces and his thin, insignificant body.

The mechanic stubbed at a meaty chin with a fat thumb. Cob imagined the man must think him slow.

"Good car, bad engine," the mechanic repeated. "Like a good woman with an evil heart. Know what I mean, son? One that looks good while doing you wrong." Cob nodded. "But nothing that will get the best of us. No, sir. Isn't a woman or engine can't be fixed by the right man with his right hand."

"How long?" Cob asked.

The mechanic leaned his heavy body on the Plymouth, which sagged under the weight. "Two days, if parts be cooperative."

"How much?"

The mechanic started to mumble something, dropped his gaze, and Cob realised the man was honest and had an honest man's aversion to bartering.

"I need it tomorrow," Cob said. The mechanic raised his eyes. Cob raised his wallet and opened it. He removed a series of bills without counting them and placed them on the hood of the Plymouth. "But, son…." The mechanic's dry protests stuck in his throat as his dilating pupils counted the money. His lips turned pale under a set of wiry grey whiskers.

"Tomorrow," Cob repeated. "Early morning."

"Yes, sir. But, sir," the mechanic said. Cob took a step toward the passenger's side door. "A young man like yourself should save what he earns. Should save it and…." Cob swung the door open and took out his guitar, handling it tenderly, gingerly, like one handles innocence, or one's gentlest lover. "…and…and spend it on a thing worthwhile. A thing like an education, son. That's what matters these days. An education at one of those good, big city schools. Life is not what it was when I was young. It's not just hard work. It's brains and taught trickery they want now." Cob slung the guitar over his shoulder and turned to look the mechanic in the face. "If you want to be somebody, that's what you got to have," the mechanic was saying. The money had disappeared from the hood.

"Tomorrow?" Cob asked.

"Early in the morning, sir," the mechanic said, before looking away.

Cob made toward the open garage doors, through which he could see the sunlit surface of Highway 17.

I am going to school, he thought. But I'm not going to pay and I'm not going to learn. I'm going because I want what I know I will become.

Feet planted outside, cheeks warmed by the sun, Cob stopped and beheld: morning had arrived but Black Bear Portage looked as dormant as it had an hour ago, when he'd first pulled in. The highway was empty — the highway that cut the town in half. Things cut in half often die. They twitch and bleed out. His mind began composing lyrics. But, before it could finish, his stomach whined so pathetically that Cob was forced to turn his attention to a more pressing matter:

Breakfast.

From across the highway, a restaurant beckoned. *The Tasty Totem*, its sign proclaimed; and, below, the goofy smiling face of a pipe-smoking Red Indian made it clear that: "Ours may not be the best — but they are the *only* prices in town!"

Cob shut his eyes, didn't look both ways and crossed

the street. When he was safely on the other side, when the ground felt dirt soft again, he opened them. So, fate is still on *my* side, he thought — as a logging truck thundered by only a few feet behind him. A reminder, he reassured himself, and felt the breeze tickle the hairs on the back of his neck.

Inside, *The Tasty Totem* was more restrained and less kitschy than its outside suggested.

A few patrons sat in scattered pairs, engaging in morning conversations. The bitter smell of coffee and cigarettes twirled in the air: emanating from hot cups and glass ashtrays, rising, being pushed back down by an army of slowly rotating ceiling fans. A television hung in the corner. Its black-and-white picture flickered, its sound unsynchronised and distorted. Two men sat staring at it. John F. Kennedy was on the screen. The men's mouths were open but silent. Kennedy's mouth was moving. He was reciting, "We have another sober responsibility. To recognise the possibilities of nuclear war in the missile age, without our citizens knowing what they should do and where they should go if bombs begin to fall, would be a failure of responsibility."

"Hey," another voice said. This one was undistorted and distinctly feminine. "Hey, you."

"*...I am requesting of the Congress new funds for the following immediate objectives: to identify and mark space in existing structures public and private that could be used for fall-out shelters in case of attack....*"

"Yeah, you. With the guitar. In the door."

Cob's spotlights came to rest on the face of a dark-haired woman sitting alone at a table littered with jars of —

"Jams. Jellies. Spreads. Curds. Marmalades. Mushrooms."

"*...food, water, first-aid kits and other minimum essentials for survival....*"

She was wearing a pale pink dress. Her hair fell in long, straight bunches like sheets of black Bristol over her neck and shoulders. She was leaning forward. Cob was staring, imagining strawberry jam running down, sticking to the skin of her —

"*...air-raid warning and fallout detection systems....*"

"I'm only teasing," the woman said and straightened her back, puffing out her chest, perhaps thinking she'd made Cob uncomfortable by singling him out. "Come, sit, order breakfast." She smiled not insincerely; then, turning her head, exposed the perfect tendons of her neck and yelled out, "Arnold, *customer*! Maybe you can sell him a buttered piece of toast so as he buys one of my jams you didn't."

The tendons dissolved softly back into skin. Her face returned to Cob, who hadn't moved.

"*What*!" Arnold yelled from the kitchen. "And turn off that goddamn prattle box. I heard the same goddamn speech last night, and the night before, and every goddamn night since the end of the goddamned war. Find me a fall-out-goddamned-shelter from that."

The men watching television closed their mouths. One got up and flicked off the president mid-word: "cont—"

The chair opposite the woman slid out from under her table. She motioned for Cob to have a seat. "I make my own preserves and other jarred eatables," she explained, the tips of her fingers absentmindedly caressing the slick surface of the plastic tablecloth.

"*Customer*!" she yelled at Arnold. "He's hungry. He wants breakfast. He's about to leave."

Cob unslung his guitar and leaned it against the edge of the table. The woman smelled like fruit, perspiration and sugar, he decided, lowering himself into the chair. For a moment there was silence as she studied his face and he browsed her edible wares — a silence which she broke suddenly with a spontaneous jerk of her arm.

The glass jar crashed to the floor and shattered.

"Winnie Youngblood," the woman said as her wild blueberry spread flowed out onto the *Totem's* white tiles. "Master preservationist of Black Bear Portage, and uncoordinated."

She held out her hand and Cob shook it. Her grip was firm but caring — unorthodoxly feminine. "Cob Augo, folk songwriter of Boston, Massachusetts," he introduced himself. "And fated."

She'd already eaten. He ordered eggs, bacon and a house-special coffee that tasted like burnt caramel.

As he shovelled the food into his mouth, washing it down with flavoured caffeine whenever his throat felt textured and parched — making sure not to seem too famished, too eager — he told tales about his journey, his Plymouth, the timeline and the one day he could afford to lose, here, all while keeping silent, mental track of the precision with which her lips twitched before she smiled and the way her nails, groomed to perfect, polished curves, tapped on the metal lids of jars to emphasise favourite words and phrases, and how soft her shoulders, now hidden beneath her dress, must look when she wasn't wearing one, when she was naked, alone, relaxed.

Winnie listened and asked questions.

Cob noticed the frequency with which she blinked. He noticed, too, that as she-spoke-he-spoke, their voices and the hungry pauses between them created a kind of harmony — a music: his chewing, the rhythm; Winnie's fingernails, a beat; over which her questions and his answers became the smoothest melody.

Never had a woman made him feel this way.

He had loved, yes. But this sensation was different. Love was long-lasting and powerful. Love could cause pleasure and pain. Love enticed into sacrifice and selflessness and helped achieve fulfilment. But love was not joyous. Only music was joyous. Only creating gave joy. Here, this morning, Winnie was making him feel the way only an audience and his guitar had ever made him feel.

"I'm going north around Lake Superior and through Port Arthur," he answered, "because that's where I was born."

"When was the last time you went back?"

"I haven't."

"Why did you leave?"

"I was fifteen."

The conversation expanded in ripples: and what about Boston — where had the journey started? "Club 47." Had she heard of it? She hadn't. "And Woody Guthrie, Pete Seeger?" No and no, and California was but an orange Hollywood fantasy and Massachusetts impossible to spell. "And what about you, Cob Augo?" Her eyes opened wide. "Are you real, or are you just a fantasy, too?"

His teeth broke through a strip of crispy bacon.

They both snickered.

Soon his plate was empty and the taste of coffee was fading from his lips, the restaurant's front doors swung open, swung closed, and tables saw patrons come and disappear, yet, still, they sat and talked. From his favourite pair of pants to how he'd learned to play guitar, from nylons to steel, six strings to twelve, to Christmas memories and how each had lost their virginity.

"Tell me the end of it," Winnie said abruptly.

The needle scratched the record.

The music stopped.

The sentence was too direct. Their melody tripped over its own undone shoelaces. Winnie stopped tapping on the tops of her jars. And, just like that, Cob found himself back in the only restaurant in a backward Ontario town called Black Bear Portage killing time until a dull grey-haired mechanic cured whatever disease was festering inside the engine of his ugly '56 Savoy.

The end.

"The California end of it," Winnie said. "What's in Berkeley? That's where you're going. You told me that. I want to know what happens when you get there."

"I become famous."

Winnie exploded with laughter —

Cob's jaws tightened.

— which she suppressed into an echoing, diminishing scoff. "I'm sorry. I didn't mean to make fun of you." She put her hand on his. Her skin was darker, his fingers longer. "I suppose I laughed because I don't understand how someone can simply become famous." She smiled. "But, remember, I only put things into jars."

"Folk is the future of music. Berkeley is the future of folk," Cob blurted out, hurt. "And I have gigs booked. I met a man in Boston at a club. He's given me dates in all the right coffee houses. Because that's what they drink in Berkeley. Coffee. They don't sell alcohol. And everyone drinks the coffee and stays up late and actually listens to the words you're singing." His excitement seethed. "All I need is to show up on time and play." He grabbed the neck of his guitar, which was still leaning against the table. "I just need to play *my songs* on *this guitar* and, if I do, nothing else matters."

"Cob Augo. *Fated*," she said.

"You don't believe in fate?" he shot back.

Winnie stood up from the table. "Come," she said. "You have one day to spare before you become famous. Come with me. I want to show you something."

(*"Arnold*, make sure nobody touches my jars!")

Winnie led and Cob and his guitar followed, out of the *Tasty Totem* and down a narrow gravel lane that cut away, perpendicular, to Highway 17 and away from Black Bear Portage.

The lane led into the forest. Its gravel soon became dirt, needles and decomposing leaves. Tire marks remained faintly visible in sporadic patches of dried mud. "Where are we going?" Cob asked.

"Home," Winnie said.

"Do you have a car?" Cob asked.

"I don't drive," Winnie said.

He struggled to keep pace with her long strides. He struggled to keep his eyes off her long legs. She wore bulky brown homemade boots that didn't go at all with her pink dress, the loose ends of which bounced hypnotically off the insides of her knees as she walked. Lower, her calves flexed; her calves slackened. The dress had a simple cut that hid most of her figure, but at least from the knees to the ankles she was bare. Cob's eyes didn't discriminate between bare skin and covered. They made out the shape of her ass through the dress. They studied the folds in the cotton material as it gathered around her hips. And they marvelled when, in the intermittent streams of late morning sunlight flashing through the foliage, the black hair sliding across her back teased black and flirted with blue.

Winnie turned off the lane without stopping. "Shortcut," she announced. Cob stared into the forest, which threatened with shadows and hidden moisture, and tried to wonder why he kept following — why not refuse, why not turn back? But the truth was impossible to avoid. The way he'd felt in the restaurant, how Winnie had made him feel: he wanted to feel that way again. To feel joy with her again. If only one more time.

"Are there bears out here?" he asked.

"Of course," she said. "Black ones, and wolves." And took several steps forward, which Cob dutifully aped. Winnie looked as comfortable covered by shade, in the land of the wild creatures, as she had in the light, in the land of people. Cob felt unsure, cooler. The guitar weighed more heavily on his body here. "It's not much further. Just to the river, then across, then up the mountain." She waited for a reaction. When none came, she continued. "It's not actually a mountain," she admitted. "It's really more of a hill."

Cob heard the water before he saw it: a faint buzzing that intensified like a swarm of insects, steady without the monotony of mechanisms, always on the verge of crashing, of waves, like the string of a guitar plucked hard, once-and-forever.

The trees ended.

He emerged from amongst them and approached Winnie, who was already standing on the slick, rocky edge of the white rushing water of the ("They call it the Dead Horse.") river.

Lovely, he thought. "Because the horse could go no further," Winnie said in the direction of the opposite shore. The sun was transforming the sky into afternoon. Morning felt foreign, distant. "The rider was being pursued. When he realised that the horse was dying of thirst, heard the howling of the hunt, he dismounted, fell to his knees and prayed to the gods to save them both — to allow his escape." She stepped into the water. It rose to the tops of her boots. Cob remained where he stood. "On hearing his prayers, the gods granted his wish. And the rider became the river." Another step forward: the surface surrounded her calves. "The horse drank and was refreshed, and the pursuers passed. But the horse lived a long and unhappy riderless life until, one day, passing the river once more, it fell in and drowned."

Winnie's boot slid — but she threw out her arms in time to keep her balance.

Downriver, something smashed into a jutting rock.

"Winnie!" Cob called out.

Her body looked magical walking on the water. "What are you doing?" he asked. But she couldn't hear him. She was already halfway across and the torrent's growl was too loud. Yet, for all the noise, its foamy claws still reached no higher than her calves.

Three, four, a dozen more steps, the last few conquered at a skip, and she was safely on the other side.

She spun, the wind whipped, snapped at her hair, she was laughing, her dark boots dripped water. "Come on!" she yelled. He could see the shapes of the words on her lips more clearly than he could hear them.

"That horse story doesn't make any sense," he yelled back.

"I made it up."

The wind pushed her pink dress against her brown body and, for the first time, he saw the outline of her stomach, her breasts, the triangular space between her thighs. He wanted to cross the river as badly as he'd wanted anything — *almost*: he wanted it almost as much as he wanted Berkeley.

"Take off your shoes if you're too civilised," she called. "And don't worry. There's a path. Just stay on the rocks."

"I don't swim!"

Her shore was fifty paces from his but every step seemed undefeatable.

She sat and took off her boots. "Don't swim. Walk."

He hesitated. He waited. But the Dead Horse River paid no attention and provided no clues, merely seething and frothing as before. The forest seemed to nudge him from behind.

"Are you afraid, Cob Augo?" Winnie asked from the opposite side of the world. Seated, she'd placed her bare feet on the warm Canadian Shield, spread her legs, and hugged her knees. A pair of lavender panties peeked out from under her dress. "If you believe in fate, tempt it."

Cob took the guitar from his back and grasped it with both hands for comfort as much as balance. The air about him spun. He took the first step. He felt the first, cold, volume of water seep through his shoes, soak through his socks and surround the skin of his feet. It wasn't an unpleasant sensation. The sensation muted his fear. He gained in confidence. He walked forward, over the water, step-after-step, one rock to the next, toward Winnie's spread legs, as around him the river spluttered and splashed, spraying his hands. He raised the guitar. He held it over his head. The water rose past his shoes. The path of rocks had been carefully laid. The rocks were slippery. He was halfway there, Winnie was half as far, when, without warning, the Earth *rotated* —

Directionless submersion.

The water rising noisily past his head.

Winnie dissolved.

The river flowing down his throat and into his lungs.

Sound flickering colours.

Hushed words beat against the surface of his head like the wings of so many terrified seagulls: "Stand up! Stop moving."

The gulls were right. His legs *were* bent. When he straightened them he grew and the volume returned to his ears and underfoot it was solid. His clothes drooped heavy with wetness. He spat out cold water and focussed his eyes, which, through the incoming waves, saw the blinding sun. He squinted. A hand brushed against his arm and grabbed his collar. His own hands were still raised. He was still holding the guitar above the surface of the river. As long as he saved the guitar — that was most important. Winnie's nose bumped into his chin. The nose felt warm, elastic. Her fist pulled him by the shirt, toward the shore. Although there was still water in one of his ears, the other heard well enough: "It's only up to your shoulders. Stand. You'll be fine. You fell off the path. Did you bang your head?"

He let himself be pulled out of the river without answering, put down the guitar, and collapsed onto the hard, hot shore.

Water escaped from his clothes.

Hair stuck to his face.

Winnie spread her palm on his shirt over his solar plexus and pushed gently. "I'm sorry," she said.

His stomach rose and fell, and he felt more ashamed with each successive breath. He didn't want to look her in the face. He couldn't. But her touch was comforting and he didn't want it to end, so he let his vision meander between her neck and the reddened knees supporting her body kneeling beside him. She was as wet as he was, his flannel shirt as soaked as her dress, which clung to — exposing — the feminine shapes beneath.

"It's not your fault," he said. "I slipped."

Her fingers dug into and tickled him. "I meant I'm sorry I lied about the horse and the river."

He heard her smile without seeing and remembered

the way her twitching lips always betrayed her. He wanted those lips. He wanted to see her whole body with his hands until his cheeks burned red.

She said, "You're not dying, you know. You're just a little watery, like an undercooked jam. Don't be so silently dramatic. More time on the burner is what you need."

Her tickling hand tiptoed lower.

And pulled the ends of his shirt from under his belt.

Cob propped himself up on an elbow and placed his own hand on Winnie's thigh, then started it upward, below the tightfitting cotton. The motion was anything but smooth; his damp skin sandpapered over hers, his fingerprints grazed and teased her pores. The stickiness of the dress felt like a tapestry of unshelled molluscs sliding over his knuckles.

She leaned over him, so face-to-face he couldn't look away, and kissed his lips. The kiss was brief — she pulled back quicker than he could push forward. "The black bears and the wolves," she whispered, and kissed him again as briefly, "are watching. Notorious…." This time, she let her tongue enter his mouth, before slowly extracting it, hissing, "peeping toms and perverts."

She pressed a hand to each of his smooth cheeks.

"I can taste the river on your tongue. That's what it's really called. The Tongue River. Do you want to know why?"

He purred.

"It's because —"

And he lunged at her so hard she almost fell backward and his teeth almost clattered into hers, before his tongue penetrated and sank into the warmth inside her mouth.

Her arms fell to her sides. His rose to grab her shoulders.

Which he used to lay her down upon the rocks.

"Cob Augo of Boston, I am older than you," she said as he caught his breath, looming over her. "I am married. I am a lesbian. I am the Chief's daughter. You have fallen into the river. You are dead. You are dreaming. I am a fish, and you cannot catch me."

He unbuttoned his flannel shirt and tossed it aside, leaving his upper body covered only by a nearly transparent white t-shirt. She hiked up her slightly less transparent dress and wrapped her legs around his waist until her lavender panties were touching his pants. Material rubbed against foreign material, which rubbed against white and brown and delicate skin.

As Cob kissed her over and over, there were no black bears or honest mechanics, no *Tasty Totems* or Khrushchev-Kennedys, no fall-out shelters in the event of nuclear war. There were only — they. Their moving bodies and their fluids; the wide, cracked slabs of rock beneath them, the stones scattered about; and the river — but even that was not wholly there. For now, the river was just a sound, a background hum over which they could hear themselves suppress their moaning and their gasps.

Cob spread his arms, each of which branched out into five stiff and trembling fingers. The tips of those on the left were calloused and thick-skinned from too many years of pressing strings. He placed that hand under Winnie's head to cushion the back of her skull as it bobbed against the rocks. The hair into which his fingers dug was dense and moist. The other hand, the gentler one, he turned, knuckles up, and placed on the ground to keep himself from falling. He continued kissing her; she hadn't stopped kissing him. Under that second hand, fitted perfectly into his palm, he felt a large, polished stone.

He pulled his face, his lips, away from hers as her front teeth seized at his unexpectedly fleeing tongue and she tightened her legs' grip around his waist.

He wanted more. He was feeling the joy again. He wanted to kiss her neck and her chest and the insides of her thighs, where the purple panties formed a visible, unwanted and audacious barrier. To breach that barrier, to see her pussy — that's what he most desired. What peculiar shades of brown and beige was it? How pink and purple were its insides? How was it groomed? His cock had thickened with blood. "Take off your panties," he said.

Winnie let her legs unclamp, straighten. She reached down with her hands and, scooting backward, half-pulled, half-wiggled out of her panties until they were past her ankles — from where Cob took them, crushed them in a fist and threw them into the river. The river re-saturated them instantly. Its waters ran roughly. A gust of wind rattled the branches of the shoreline trees. Winnie exhaled.

"You are older than I am," Cob said. "You are married. You are a lesbian. You are the Chief's daughter. I have fallen into the river, but I am alive. I am not dreaming. You are not a fish, and I have caught you."

He raised himself onto his knees and pulled Winnie by the legs toward him. "Lick me," she breathed. Cob flipped the bottom part of her dress onto her stomach and breasts, exposing her pussy and the smooth merge of her tummy above. It was good to expose her. But the wind today was mischievous: jealous, immature wind! It puffed and Winnie's dress ballooned, then the wind huffed, and the dress returned to its rightful place, all the way down to her knees. Cob growled, grabbed the material and, again, flipped it onto Winnie's stomach. This was one battle he would not lose. Winnie's lips twitched. Her skin learned the texture of faint goose bumps. She smiled. Cob took the stone he'd felt under his right hand and placed it on the folded material between Winnie's breasts — a paperweight. A dress-weight. They both laughed. The stone felt heavy and warm, even through two layers of cotton. Cob leaned in and kissed Winnie's chin. Then, with his nose, he drew a line from the stone to her belly button, and he finished the game by kissing her moistening pussy.

It was generally the colour of umber, with fine black hair cross-hatching and a slightly raised, slightly swollen outer labia surrounding the cocoa-toned, delicately crumpled inner lips that guarded the entrance to Winnie's pink, peeking interior. Above, a tiny and tough spherical clitoris kept soundless watch.

Cob kissed them all, sometimes one by one, sometimes

mouthfuls at a time. He kissed precisely yet greedily while his hands massaged the body to which the pussy belonged: the moving body, the bucking hips, the leg muscles pulling, the abdomen pushing, the pair of unseen lungs filling with the freshest, most unspoiled air; and the breasts, hugged by the wet dress, responding to both pleasure and gravity. He cupped and squeezed until Winnie squirmed and forced her lower body at his face. He kissed. He kissed more and more quickly until he couldn't keep up and he was forgetting to breath and — *slick* — their bodies slid out of rhythm and his nose, still blushing from its long trip from chest to sex, penetrated Winnie's vagina.

The sensation wasn't unpleasant. It was just completely unexpected. Cob pulled his face away immediately. Winnie's hips bucked several more times before realising they were bucking against air. She opened her eyes. *Where*, they seemed to ask, *did you go*? Cob's nose, a good two thirds of it, felt colder than the rest of his stunned face as he stared at hers. He didn't know what to say, what to do. But his nose must have shone in the intense sunlight because before he could decide to do anything, the edges of Winnie's lips twitched.

"Don't," Cob said, his voice slurring the words to get them out quickly enough, "laugh."

Winnie bit her lower lip. She was a good girl, an obedient girl. She wouldn't laugh. She didn't even crack a smile. The stone on her chest merely rose and, lowering her head back onto the rocks, squinting at the sky, "You fucked me with your nose," she murmured.

Cob wiped Winnie's juices off his face. His nose felt instantly warmer. He tried to appear indifferent, to bluff, but no woman had ever had his nose inside her before, and he was genuinely irritated by the idea — though he couldn't explain why — which irritated him even more, and now Winnie's shoulders and belly had started to jiggle and she had buried her face in her hands and was rocking back and forth like a child with an incurable case of the sillies.

"Don't laugh!"

He said it sternly, while thinking at the same time that it was now impossible to imagine himself singing serious songs to serious people in serious coffee houses having experienced something like this. Some events, like knee injuries for running backs or infidelity for presidential candidates, just could not be overcome. He tried imagining Woody Guthrie's bony nose in some woman's cootch. It was undoable. That crop of wild hair and —

He started jiggling, too. "Stop it and be serious," he warned, his voice joyfully staccato. "Or I'll do it again, I swear."

"I dare you!"

He crawled onto her and they were both laughing. He was trying to wipe his nose against her face, which she still covered with her hands, which were — at the same time — attempting to shield herself and swat him playfully away.

To counter, he fell on top of her like a sack of sudden potatoes. The impact knocked some of the wind out of her. His chest flattened her breasts. But she kept laughing: "I dare you. I dare you."

Only their wet clothes and the warm stone was between them. It poked at his sternum and the more he laughed the more it poked. And the more she laughed, the more he laughed; and she was laughing more and more, until he didn't know whether to give in to the laughter, too, or sit up and rub his aching bone. Finally, he did neither. Finally, he moved his body down until his chin was in her belly button, and tickled her with it. She kicked her feet in pleasure. He grabbed and held down her legs. She was biting her lower lip again, her eyes were shut. Further down he went, his chin flicking her clit, catching on the skin of her pussy; his chin stopping, nose hovering a quarter of an inch away, and he blowing through it, the unexpected air sending Winnie into another fit of giggles. His arms barely managed to contain her wild, imprisoned legs.

"Don't blow your nose at me. Fuck me with it," she said. "Pinocchio," she said. "Liar, liar," she said. And relaxed her body in the most comfortable nose-fucking position she could assume, laughter still flitting inside her stomach like butterflies. Cob couldn't believe what he was seeing. Such a beautiful pussy but such languor — expecting him to do all the work, waiting for his nose to enter her and do what? Breathe? Squish around? All while she laughed and enjoyed herself at his expense. It was demeaning, a blow against his manhood. Cob Augo was not a kept boy. He was not a toy. He was a nose-fucker once and by accident. To be the same twice, and by a woman's choice….

He lifted the stone gently from her dress.

If she wanted something put in her, he'd give her something. Strange for stranger, unexpected for unusual — a substitution. He chuckled at his own ingenuity. But somewhere deeper and more honest, he marvelled at how playful she was making him feel, at how little he knew about her, how little time they'd spent together, yet how at-ease they were together.

Her hips bobbed, inviting company. Her empty pussy called for an occupier.

He let the stone travel from finger to finger as he imagined reaction after reaction: shock followed by humiliation followed by humility, and *he* would be the one laughing, but then he would also be the one to kiss her and tell her that she was the most wonderful woman he'd ever known and she would confess that she'd never had a stone in her before and she would say it felt odd but enjoyable and he would feel special for being her first. He even invented the corny phrase he would use. "Am I the first man you've ever been stoned with?"

"What," Winnie moaned.

He hadn't meant to say it out loud. He positioned the stone at the entrance to her pussy. A few hairs scratched its stony surface. Water, the river's perhaps, had polished it to near perfect smoothness. His hand started to shake. He was rushing. Why was he so nervous?

"Cob?"

The edge of the stone disappeared between Winnie's

inner labia, her excitement coating it, making it sticky and dark. He'd pushed it in with his forefingers. Now he fanned his fingers out on her thighs and belly and put his thumbs against the stone.

"What on earth...."

His thumbs pushed, the stone slid, Winnie's pussy swallowed it up, but of all the possible reactions that his imagination had devised, none were:

Winnie leapt to her feet!

Her knees barely avoided making violent impact with Cob's head as he bobbed out of the way. Before he could right himself, Winnie was already wearing one boot and lacing up the other. Cob was still wearing his shoes. They were fine shoes, but squelchy. "Winnie," he said without knowing what to say next and ended up saying nothing. He picked up his guitar instead, slung it over his shoulder and took a few squelchy steps toward her, but she turned before he could look at her face, so he followed — squelch, squeak, squish. The sounds, indecent in their suction, turned him on. He realised he had an erection. The wet shoes and the erection made walking difficult. He couldn't keep up. "Winnie," he called after her again. He'd left his flannel shirt behind but there wasn't time to go back for it now. Winnie disappeared into the forest.

Cob disappeared after her, waddling like a duck. The buzz of the river faded. The trees cast their shadows. Catching up to her to say he was sorry was one thing — and, truth be told, he didn't quite know how to do that yet. He'd burn up from shame, but right now he also needed a guide. He didn't know where he was. He needed to eventually get back to Black Bear Portage. "Slow down, please," he yelled. But, if she heard him, she didn't let it show.

The ground sloped upwards. Cob tripped over a root and covered a dozen feet at a crawl before becoming a biped again. But even bipeds are primitive, he knew, because all he could think about was whether the stone was still in Winnie's pussy. "I'm sorry," his conscience and manners wanted to tell her while his cock was telling him that his neck needed to bend-and-peek and his legs should learn to manoeuvre more efficiently. "You threw her panties into the river," his cock reasoned. "Therefore, she is not wearing panties. Therefore, her pussy is unprotected. Capture her. Position her. Enter her."

"Winnie!"

But Winnie passed behind a tree and vanished into the shadows.

Half an hour later, Cob, out-of-breath, conquered the crest of a hill and cast his forlorn and horny gaze upon a clearing. In the middle of the clearing stood a house — small, white. Attached to the front of the house, a porch. On the porch, sitting on the railing, legs dangling, black hair flowing, was Winnie. She wasn't wearing the pink dress anymore.

Cob fell to his knees. "I'm sorry," he pleaded. His lungs wheezed rust. "It was wrong of me."

Winnie slid off the railing and went inside.

Cob hobbled up to the front door. It was locked, but at least his erection was almost gone. He knocked. "Yes," came the voice from inside.

"Oh, for the sake of all that's good, open up. I don't have any more stones." Silence was followed by the subtle creaking of floorboards.

"Who is it? I'm a woman alone and I've just been chased by a pervert."

Cob sat back on his heels on the porch. He finger-picked a melody from the strings of his guitar.

A minute later, the lock clicked and the door swung open. "Hello, stranger," Winnie said. "You play beautifully." Her lips twitched, before opening and smiling at the same time, and she added, "for such a pervert."

Cob felt relief, immense and sudden relief. He wouldn't die in the wild after all. Mostly, though, he just wanted to see Winnie again. He took a step toward the door — but found the way barred unexpectedly by a slender brown arm.

"Excuse me," Winnie said. "But you are soaking wet and I will not have you dripping water all over my house." Cob blinked — three times. "What I mean is, *take off your clothes, musician.*"

Cob removed both shoes, unbuckled his belt and let his pants drop to the porch floor. He then pulled his t-shirt over his head in such haste that the collar caught and dishevelled his hair, before tossing the whole collection into an unfolded pile by the door. Winnie left the shoes, but picked up the rest. She remained barring the doorway.

"May I come in now?" Cob asked.

"Your undergarment is still wet, musician," she said.

He became aware of the burgeoning erection faintly visibly through his wet boxer shorts. The word "undergarment" had stirred up ideas. Winnie was wearing a blue dress of the same cut as her pink one, but her boots were off and feet bare. As she squeezed her unpainted toes, Cob wondered what else was bare. Had she put on a fresh pair of panties, a dry bra? She hadn't been wearing a bra before. If he squinted, he could almost make out the faint outlines of nipples —

Winnie cleared her throat.

"Turn around," Cob attempted to command.

But the attempt failed. Winnie placed a hand on her hip. Cob's wet clothes looked like a ball of colours lodged into the three-sided space between her forearm, bicep and side. "You put a stone inside my vagina," she said, emphasising each word. "Now strip."

Cob dug his thumbs under the elastic band at the top of his boxers, stretched, and stepped out of them into complete nakedness. Winnie added the boxers to her ball of Cob's other clothing.

"I'll make sure they dry," she said, looking at his not-quite-flaccid penis. She was straining to suppress a smirk. He was trying not to flush. As far as he could remember, he'd never been naked with a woman in the middle of a forest before. "You may step into the living room — it's the one with the fireplace, to your immediate left — and wait for me. I'll be with you shortly." She started, then stopped. "And don't touch anything."

The living room was small and cosy. It smelled of sugar and berries, leather, kerosene and wood. Shelves overflowing with old photographs, papers, crafts, tools and knives, and other, sometimes unascertainable, bric-a-brac lined the walls. Several tall windows let in blocks of dull sunlight through foggy, opaque panes. The overriding atmosphere was one of stillness, broken only by the many, slowly gliding particles of dust.

There was also the fireplace. It was imposingly solid even when cold. But the fireplace was hardly the room's dominant feature. What first caught Cob's attention as he crossed the threshold — what made him pause, made his heart beat twice — was another object, a once-living one: a large black bearskin rug that covered a sizable portion of the wooden floor. The dead bear's massive head, maw open, teeth sharp, stared blankly ahead at nothing.

Cob took a seat on a cushion on the floor, making sure to keep his feet away, just in case.

After rubbing some warmth into his nude body, he started to glance around. Masculine faces reflected his gaze from several of the photographs. Perhaps Winnie *was* married — a thought that made the presence of the knives slightly disconcerting. He held his breath and listened for a suggestion either way, but the only sound was silence, no marital conversation, no man's heavy stomp — broken finally by the shriek of a whistling kettle.

He was eyeing a raccoon-tailed hat sitting atop a stack of books when Winnie walked in, carrying two steaming cups.

"I made coffee," she said.

He held out his hand and waited for her to pass him one of the cups. She raised an eyebrow. "Do you think I'll drink it for you, too? Stand up."

"I'm naked," he said.

"I'll get you something to wear in a second. Just take the coffee." Impatience dripped from her voice.

He stood without covering up and took from her the heavy, oversized mug. It felt pleasantly warm in his hands. She sipped from hers and pointed with her chin toward one of the shelves. "There," she said. "I saw you looking at it." He didn't understand. "You wanted clothing, didn't you?" He followed with his eyes and realised her chin was pointing in the direction of the raccoon hat. "What?" But, instead of answering, she took three strides, perched briefly on a wicker chair, retrieved the hat from its shelf, and put it crookedly on Cob's head.

"There. You're not naked anymore."

Unclothed and in a Davy Crockett cap, it was a new low. Cob lifted his cup to his lips and took a long drink of coffee. At least the coffee wouldn't make fun of him.

Something in the cup rattled.

He looked down. The liquid looked up, dark and opaque. It had tasted like coffee, but.... He shook the cup again.

Another rattle.

"Why don't you play me one of your songs," Winnie said.

"What's in the coffee?" Cob said back.

"You know what's in the coffee."

Even the raccoon's tail seemed to bristle. "How would I know?" he barked, but was immediately aware that the question was autonomic. He did know. He'd known from the very first rattle.

"Because we're crazy in the same ways, Cob Augo."

He felt his erection returning.

"Did you…inside…?" He nearly choked, swallowing an excess of saliva and a few unimportant words. "All this time?"

"Do you need to ask to know?"

He took another drink.

"When I was reaching for your hat, you tried to look up my dress," she said.

That wasn't quite true. He'd been staring through her dress, at her ass, though that defence was hardly noble. Plus, he did want to know if she was still wearing panties. And he would have gladly looked up her dress had there been more time. And, really, how much more embarrassed could he possibly be. "I tried," he admitted. "Unsuccessfully."

"Do you want another chance?"

His mind was stunned. His cock nodded feverishly.

"I'll make you a deal. I will let you look up my dress if you play a song for me. My only condition is that the song is new — a song that no one's heard before."

"Agreed," he said, and tried lowering himself, cross-legged, onto the cushion on the floor.

Winnie tut-tutted him into an awkward semi-crouch instead. "That's my spot. You can sit on Edward." Her arm pointed at the bearskin rug. "He's fluffy and warm and he doesn't bite — anymore." Neither Winnie's voice nor the bear's facial expression suggested a desire to be disobeyed. Cob did as instructed.

The bear's fur was long and softer than anything he'd experienced. Sitting on it was like melting into a layer of warm butter as hundreds-of-thousands of individual hairs, the same midnight colour as Winnie's, rose against his skin and tickled the much coarser hairs covering his own body.

"I'll bring your guitar," she said.

But Cob understood that, for once, he wouldn't need his guitar. It was as obvious as the rattle of the stone in his coffee cup. In the *Tasty Totem*, Winnie had made him feel joy because he'd felt a common creation with her. This was the next step. If it was too literal, so be it. He had no pride or pretence left to lose. She'd stripped him of those as easily as of his clothes. "I don't need my guitar," he said.

He anticipated her imminent protests. "I promised you a song. I'll give you a song." Finally he'd caught her off guard with something! Watching her struggle to understand was a happy novelty. Maybe he wasn't quite the fool in the coonskin hat that, inevitably, he looked. He went on, "But one condition deserves another, and my condition is that a new song deserves a new guitar, and as my guitar, I choose you, Winnie Youngblood."

She downed the rest of her coffee in one gulp.

He set his aside.

"And how exactly does one become a guitar?" she asked.

"One pictures it — clearly, with details. Then one attempts to create the picture with reality."

She scoffed. "I can't do that. I can't picture myself as a guitar. It's absurd."

"Have you seen a guitar?"

"Of course." Cob's cock licked its lips.

"Then picture it."

Winnie leaned against the wall. The blue material between her breasts tightened. "When I make a marmalade or a sauce, there's a recipe I follow. Instructions. Can't you picture it for me and tell me the instructions?"

"We're creating," Cob said, "not recreating. The first marmalade wasn't made from a recipe."

When Winnie didn't react, Cob grabbed his cup and lifted it to the heavens. "Cheers!"

"And what are you toasting?"

"The Dead Horse River. The ridiculous, the dreamers, and the losing of self-restraint." He smiled so wide the corners of his mouth hurt. "I'm naked, save for a raccoon on my head. I have an erection I can't get rid of, and I'm sitting on a bear named Edward. For the last few minutes, I've been drinking coffee that tastes vaguely like your pussy. Spare me if you feel a little self-conscious."

She dropped her shoulders and came toward him like a puppy-done-wrong.

She sat beside him on Edward's soft black fur, and leaned her head against his shoulder. "If you're sorry for putting a stone in me, I'm sorry for making you get naked and wear a coonskin headpiece." She scratched her forehead. "But I think the truth is that neither of us truly wants to apologise. Thank God for that." And she dropped her head onto his knees, then pulled herself forward and rotated her body until her back was across his thighs and both her head and legs were dangling off his crossed knees.

Cob responded by slipping his left forearm under her head, propping up her neck, and rubbing her stomach with his other hand, before moving it cautiously beneath her dress and realising — much later than he would have liked — that she wasn't wearing panties after all.

"I picture myself as a slide guitar," she said.

He put two fingers in her mouth to shut her up. "And when you picture this slide guitar, does it talk?" She answered by sucking his fingers.

He enjoyed the sensation for a few seconds before removing his fingers from her mouth and threading them into as much of her hair as possible. She let him. He brought the hair over her face until she was faceless and the strands were solid black and reaching to the bottoms of her ribs. "One," he counted, separating one-sixth of the strands into a band. "Two," and another sixth became another band, and all the way until "Six," when all of Winnie's hair was divided, and the strings of Cob's guitar were complete.

Wedges of skin and two quiet eyes peeked out from in between.

Cob bent his body low and wrapped his left arm under Winnie's neck as far as it would go, until his nimble fingers were able to touch all six bands of hair. Carefully, his breath held, he pressed one finger on each of the second-and third-closest strings, as his right hand slid between Winnie's unsteady thighs. "E minor," he said. Winnie moaned. He immediately shifted to a different chord. "D minor. This one sounds brighter." Winnie moaned more brightly. "And —" His fingers crawled up her torso, deft and gentle. "G major." Winnie's moan became a deep kitten's purr. Cob squeezed flesh. His fingers returned to E*m*. The resulting grunt warmed his cheeks. "That's not how you play a slide guitar, of course. But this is my first time, so you'll have to excuse me." She offered no reaction. She had become the instrument.

Cob played a simple blues progression, followed by a traditional Appalachian ballad. Winnie purred and twisted, squirmed, hummed and, gutturally groaning, liquefied into the appropriate sounds. He played a pop song and she puffed. He played a song for lovers and she sighed.

Over time, the bands of Winnie's hair began to come

apart, to blend, the guitar strings frayed, but it made no difference. Cob's fingers still twirled and flew. And, as they did, his other hand began to add a beat — first tapping on Winnie's stomach, then slapping against her thigh — while the familiar youthful shapes of rock-and-roll spread out across her breasts.

And as the music became wilder, less refined, so did Cob's motions. His fingers pressed harder, his fingernails dug deeper. On some notes he pinched. On others he vibrated. And on others still he slid gracefully from the top of the neck to its bottom, pointer finger barring, ring finger rhythmically repeating. Winnie's breath quickened, her pulse doubled. Cob experimented, recalled and improvised. He tapped and he counted, treble-clefed and quarter-noted, and composed until, closing his eyes, he forgot and felt and finally knew that the music he was creating was as real as any he had ever made.

Winnie's moans grew louder.

More passionate.

Uncontrolled.

Cob's right hand crawled between her quivering legs.

His cock tick-tocked, a metronome.

The bands of hair across Winnie's body were a ruffled mess. The hair between her thighs was wet. Over the former, like chord shapes he floated; into the latter he greedily descended. His fingertips dipped and moistened. He pushed those fingertips, those whole fingers, inside Winnie's pussy. She moaned in D*m*. He removed them; Winnie quivered, a perfectly realised F.

He petted. He teased. He penetrated. He....

Strummed.

And she reacted and murmured. She blubbered, moaned, groaned, grunted and — finger-fucked beyond all measure of decency — exploding and screaming, unwilling, *unable* to stop herself, she came.

Cob's hands stopped moving.

Winnie's body vibrated to stillness in the murky sunlight.

Particles of dust drifted through the air.

And yet music reverberated between the walls even as Edward the Bear's expressionlessness persisted and Cob fixed the raccoon hat, resting dangerously crooked, on his head while Winnie rolled off his legs, onto her stomach, onto the black fur.

The music was louder than the silence.

Outside, somewhere in the world beyond, lightning flashed, followed by the faint crash of distant thunder. Cob realised there were no clocks in the room. Theirs was a time out of mind, a secret place. He slapped his erect cock to the side and watched it rebound to attention. Never had he made a woman cum — at least not like today, not for certain.

He picked up his cup and drank the rest of the lukewarm coffee, exposing the stone, which he let fall into his palm before placing it back into the cup:

Rattle.

Winnie stirred. She got to her knees; then, slowly,

rose to her feet. She swayed to the music. Cob watched her sway and felt jealous of Edward the Bear and Arnold the Cook and Dull the Mechanic and anyone else who'd ever seen Winnie or fantasised about her. He even felt jealous of John the President, because who could say he'd never, in his dreams, imagined Winnie swaying to the music just like so. "Cob Augo," she said, slipping easily out of her blue dress. "You are not really from 1961 and neither am I."

He tried to speak.

"Shh," she said. She swayed, she neared, she put a finger to his lips. "Don't say words, for this is the best part. This is the part where I fuck you."

And she pushed his chest.

He let himself fall backward onto black fur.

The racoon hat dropped off his head.

When he was as defenceless as an overturned beetle and his cock was the tallest part of his body, she squatted over him with her legs spread and, slowly, began to descend. Cob understood the masculine fascination with rockets. Winnie's pussy touched the head of his penis — its hairs raked his delicate skin, the soft surplus of flesh took him between its lips like her hands had taken his cheeks. He growled. Or Edward growled. As much as he wanted to let off his boosters and explode upward, he also wanted — wanted more — to make this moment last for eternity.

The head of his cock disappeared inside Winnie.

The veins entangling its shaft pulsated with hot blood. Caffeine swam inside. He wanted more coffee, more liquid. Her pussy squished and squelched like a bowl of chocolate pudding devoured by a greedy child with a silver spoon. He felt the pussy devouring *him*. He felt her weight and her wetness arrive at the root — his thighs, his belly. He was in her completely. He had her; she had him. If she were a moon, he would have planted a flag in her lunar soil, ripped off his oxygen mask, cast his radio equipment into the coldness of space and breathed in whatever atmosphere she had, hoping for, but oblivious to, his life lasting for no more than a few indescribable seconds.

She leaned forward. Her hair fell onto his face, his chest. She started moving her hips. He felt the various angles of her mass. His cock slid in, slid out. He opened his mouth with no intention of saying anything — just to breathe. She licked the row of his upper teeth. He locked his knees and grabbed her upper body, taking hold of her breasts. She bounced; he squeezed. She squeezed; he thrust — past the constricting, grasping tightness of her pussy.

The pale handprints on her chest dissolved into the colour of honey.

She stroked his face with a snake's tongue.

He kneaded her ass with needy hands.

And when he couldn't take it anymore, when his grip was possessive, breath savage and mind devolved past primitive man's invention of fire, she let up — slowed, lightened and then rose; suddenly massless, she floated up and his cock felt as wet and cool as his nose had once, a long, long time ago by a roughly running, loudly buzzing river.

She left the room.

His cock punctuated the sentence.

He pictured her crying, overcome with emotion. He wanted to comfort her like a friend. He pictured her laughing, and wanted to choke her like an enemy. He imagined her as she was and as she had been and as she would be till death do us part and all he wanted was to fuck her again, to keep fucking her....

He pulled the racoon hat back onto his head.

"What's your favourite berry?"

Her voice was muffled. The question sounded sincere. "I'm all out of strawberry, but blackcurrant is delicious on summer evenings."

She reappeared carrying a pair of glass jars filled with two different colours of jam. "I recommend this one," she said, and held up the darker of the two. "It's less sweet, more tart, goes well with most anything. But it's up to you." Naked, she looked less girlish, more womanly than she had clothed. "Which do you prefer to taste like, musician?"

"I agree with expert opinion," he said.

She lay the other jar on a shelf, between two hunting knives and an antique silver bracelet, and sat beside him. "Open it," she said. He untwisted the lid with a thump. The fruity aroma escaped up into his nostrils. Winnie took back the jar, stuck her hand inside — her wrist was just small enough to fit — and scooped out a handful of black currant jam; which she proceeded to rub on Cob's nude, sweating chest. Before he could react, she rubbed trails across his face, then his thighs, then licked up the taste from all three parts of his body. She stuck out a stained tongue. "Try some." He set loose his tongue on hers. She wrapped her fingers around his hard cock, which, when their kiss was finished, she covered in an entire second helping of black currants until it glistened and dripped, gooey, over his testicles.

When she leaned down to clean up, he made sure her head stayed below. She kissed her way up the shaft of his cock. He gathered her hair and held it away from her face because he wanted to see. Her teeth pressing into his skin, her eyes staring into his. Her tongue became a pillow for his cock. He felt the ribbing on the roof of her mouth, felt her saliva thicken, bubble and, delicately, burst. She was swallowing the jam. She was sucking him. He tightened the fist squeezing her hair. A few streaks of rain slashed at the windows. His muscles contracted and toes curled. The raccoon hat fell forward off his head, onto Winnie's. He pressed down on it — the hat, the head — until dark purple spit flowed out from between lips-and-cock. Winnie gasped. Cob pushed deeper, further, harder.

And orgasmed.

His semen mixed with the black currant jam and, together, the salty-sweet concoction went down Winnie's throat.

Cob let go of hat, hair and head.

More tiny fists of drizzle tapped at the windowpanes.

"Your guitar," Winnie said and thunder rolled and Cob realised that by this time tomorrow he'd be gone, would be another six hundred miles along Highway 17, six hundred closer to Berkeley and six hundred further away from Black Bear Portage. "It's still on the porch. You should bring it in. The grey clouds are coming. The storm will be here before nightfall."

"It's not dark yet," he said.

She said, "But it's getting there."

Outside, the warm air was stagnant and the atmosphere had turned to early evening pale. A damp wind hung like a towel that wouldn't dry. Cob looked around. The forest revealed nothing; there was nothing to see but the forest. But he knew that beyond lay fog and fame, Berkeley and all the days still to come, so he picked up his guitar and went into the living room, where Winnie was lying naked on her back, big eyes forced open, a question forming on their glassy surfaces. "Tell me," she whispered to the ceiling, "what's so special about that guitar?"

Cob put the guitar down and laid himself on the floor beside her. "It's the guitar I saw," he said, "when I pictured myself famous. It's one of the clear details."

She finished the thought for him. "And now you have to create the picture with reality."

He put his palm on her forehead. "You think I'm naïve."

She said, "I'm afraid you'll get hurt." He felt the muscles on her head move. "Do you know why I brought you out here — what I wanted to show you?"

He didn't say anything.

She said, "I wanted you to see the house that my grandfather died in, that my father died in, and that one day I will die in." The distant thunder rolled closer.

"After a long and happy life, unlike the horse," he said but she didn't hear.

"I'm afraid fate is not what you think it is, Cob Augo. To you, fate is hope. To me, it's knowing that there's not going to be anything else."

He turned on his side and hugged her but she felt far away.

After a few minutes, the glaze disappeared from her eyes, she smiled and said, "I'm babbling like an old woman."

She stood up, leaving Cob alone on the floor. "I'm also not being a good hostess. The darkness is getting inside. Forgive me, I'll get a lantern going." She took her blue dress from the floor and walked out of the room — out of his life, Cob felt; and the feeling twisted his heart. He stood too, touched his guitar and imagined all the music they would make together, how good it would make him feel. She was wrong about fate. He wasn't wrong about anything.

She came back carrying his clothes. "They're dry," she said. He took them without wanting to put them on. His nakedness didn't embarrass him anymore. "I'm out of oil." She held up an empty paraffin lamp. "But there's more in the shed. I won't be long."

"Do you want me to go with you?" he asked.

"No," she said.

"It's raining," he said.

But she was already out the door.

He waited for a minute, several. Rain pitter-pattered harder. Ink dripped down the windows. Lightning turned the sky on, turned the sky off. He waited for several more minutes, opened the door and walked outside.

Raindrops splattered on the porch railing.

Cob's clothes got wet again.

Barefoot, he marched over wet grass and soft soil in no particular direction, squinting through the gloom and precipitation, searching for a shed — searching for Winnie — as mud cushioned his heels and surrounded his toes. Streams of water fell from overflowing leaves. Already, it was gathering in shallow puddles. He looked for footprints in the ground around them, but found none. The gap between lightning and thunder was closing.

"Cob."

Winnie's voice.

He wiped his face and stared ahead. Through the haze, he saw a bobbing light. On the other side of the mist, she was holding the lit paraffin lamp and waving to him. "Come on, Cob!"

He ran toward her.

He touched the bend of her elbow.

Together, they skipped over the surface of the wet

grass and through the clinging mud, her lamp lighting their way, both of them starting to laugh, both slipping and sliding until, finally, they fell into the shelter of the shed.

The shed was aluminium, large and filled with crates and other old things. Winnie hung the paraffin lamp on a hook. Its unstable light flowed across the walls, the floor and their laughing faces. It flowed across Winnie's body and Cob wanted to feel the joy again, as thunder roared above and the rain beating against the roof of the shed was so loud he could barely hear her speak: "It's raining," she said. "Don't leave me."

He remembered the first time he'd heard her voice and couldn't believe it was less than half-a-day ago. Back then, before, in the *Tasty Totem* where John F. Kennedy was reassuring about fallout shelters and he was hungry and saw her smiling from behind a table full of glass jars:

There was a horrible crash —

Of lightning.

They'd broken one of the jars. The wild blueberry spread had stained the tile floor and he shook her hand. "Winnie Youngblood," she'd introduced herself. It was a name that twelve hours ago he didn't know. It was a name that in twelve lifetimes he wouldn't forget.

They stepped toward each other.

"The forest is coming down," he said, as she said, "I hope the dry trees don't catch fire." This morning, the lake had burned and for a few seconds he'd been driving into its flames. "It's not a fire," he said. From above, the rain pounded on the brittle, echoing aluminium. The shed bent and creaked. "It's nuclear war," he whispered, grabbing her hips and holding them tightly against himself. Her body squirmed, struggled against his grip. "I want to see — I want to look outside!" But she couldn't break through. "It's better if you don't. We should stay inside until it's over." Tears were streaming down her face. "So this is how it ends?" she said. The paraffin lamp spun; Winnie cast a monstrous shadow on the wall. Cob dug his fingers into her dress, her flesh. "I don't know. Tomorrow we'll wake up and if the world still exists, then…." She shoved a fist deep into his mouth.

"Tonight is the last night."

Cob's mouth feasted on the shapes of her knuckles. His heart pounded in tune with her ragged, sobbing breath. "So, let me go outside," she syncopated.

He didn't want to let her go anywhere. He wanted to keep her close, to tell her something, *anything*; but her fingers depressed his tongue, distorting his intention into a gurgle.

"No more words."

She reached back. Metal clanged against metal.

For a second, his mouth was empty, "Winnie," he managed to say — before tasting the flavour of leather. Her hands moved quickly, the knot tightened against the lump on the back of his skull, the buckle jangled. He was dumbfounded. She'd gagged him with an old utility belt. He felt the metal rings and hooks where the tools should have been, resting on his wet shirt.

She petted his hair.

She massaged his shoulders.

He let his arms drop from the sides of her hips.

She moved toward the closed shed door. The blue dress stuck to her body like paint.

"Fated," she said, and reached for the outside.

Cob reached for her.

But around them was too much noise. He couldn't focus. He saw an old leash, shears, tin cans, the busted body of an acoustic guitar. He smelled leather and Winnie and moist wood. The cotton of her dress escaped from between his fingertips. He bit down on the work belt until leathery juice leaked into his gums. *To catch her and to keep her.* Truncated: *To catch and to keep.* Repeated: *to catch and to keep, to catch and to keep.* His mind rolled numb. He wanted to rub his knuckles into his eyes, into his brain. He'd been driving for too long. The next place he came to, he would stop and drink coffee and eat scrambled eggs every morning with Winnie....

He leapt.

His chest crashed into Winnie's back. Hers crashed into the door. Together, they fell; Cob on top of Winnie, they wrestled. Her face: stone carved determination; his: overheating. Grunting, she bit at the veins of his exposed wrist. He separated her wrists and pinned them to the shed floor, tore the leash from its place on the wall, and wound it round one wrist, tightened, followed by the other, tightened, followed by the sight of her twitching lips. "Cob Augo," she said — he ripped the belt gag from his mouth, it dropped to his neck. The rest of her sentence dissolved into his mouth as he attacked and consumed her, exhaling hot breath, passionately kissed her.

He kissed her until his lungs hurt.

He kissed her until the blood pulsing through his ears drowned out every other sound.

And then he broke his lips away and stood.

Winnie sat up, holding her bound wrists in front of her.

"Stand up."

She did and he picked up the pair of shears that, for decades probably, had been waiting in the corner of the shed.

"Turn around."

When she had, he forced the shears open and slid their metal along her calf, more slowly up her thigh, slicing, carefully down the other thigh, slicing, until the back of her blue dress fell away from between her legs, away from the twin, ready blades. Cob repositioned the tool, and the downside of the shears burrowed in the crevice of her buttocks.

He pressed the handles together. The blades sliced.

Slicing, they travelled upward along the spinal groove of Winnie's back.

The dress parted, uncovering skin.

Cotton crumpled and fell.

Cob put the shears back in the corner and pressed his clothed self against Winnie's nakedness.

He pulled her backward.

Then down.

Then she was on hands and knees, struggling to keep her balance on bound wrists, and he was untying one of the strings from the old acoustic guitar. "Move your legs together," he said.

When the string was free he knelt behind her and wrapped it around her ankles. As he tightened, he tuned. As he tuned, the string dug, gradually, into Winnie's flesh. Cob was fascinated to realise that even such a small place on her body had such wonderful depth.

"Does it hurt?" he asked.

"A little," she said. But he didn't loosen it.

He undressed behind her, where she couldn't see, and stroked himself while watching her shoulders dip to the floor as her ass rose in counterpoint.

When he was ready, he mounted.

They both moaned as he slid his cock across — then into — her pussy.

Cob fucked. Winnie tried fucking back, throwing her hips against, crashing into, his. But he wouldn't let her. He'd caught her, now he would keep her. He fucked harder. *Tonight was the last night.* His fucking outmuscled hers until her hips gave way and her body gave in and, pressing his chest against her back, he palmed her throat, ran his fingers through her hair, and pulled back her head. The angle of penetration shifted ever so slightly. It felt deeper. It felt good. Her skin felt smooth and slick. His cock felt snug inside her domesticated cunt. He wanted to make all of these feelings last forever. He wanted to pray to the gods to grant his wish. He wanted to be the Dead Horse River. He wanted Berkeley and concerts on elevated stages, coffee house crowds, lyrics, and the creation of music. He wanted joy. He wanted fame. He wanted to keep fucking.

And the harder he fucked, the better it felt. But the better it felt, the closer he was to orgasm. His distracted, feverishly horny mind sputtered, struggling with the problem of *by this time tomorrow I'll be gone* and *never has a woman made me feel this way* and *this is the most important journey of my life.* He was certain he wasn't wrong about anything. Yet there was something wrong with his engine, something festering inside. His body screamed. His body moaned. The gulls were clawing at his head again. The problem wasn't anything a man can fix with his right hand. The storm hailed; the hail dented the aluminium siding of the shed. Cob grunted, he gripped Winnie, his balls, tired, were rolling insufficiently along the fresh asphalt of Highway 17 —

He came.

And disappeared into the rear view.

The hail abated. The last few stones smacked into and slid off the roof. Cob was suddenly aware of the shed and everything in it: the acoustic guitar, the tin cans, the crumpled blue dress, the shears standing in the corner. He pulled out of Winnie at last, before stumbling backward and losing his balance into a pile of junk. It was louder but not nearly as bad as falling into the river.

Upon regaining his balance, he used the shears to cut through the belt around his neck and the guitar string binding Winnie's ankles. The skin on the latter was slightly raw. Next, he undid the leash tying together Winnie's wrists and handed her the ruined blue dress, in case she wanted to cover up. She handed it back, saying there was a blanket in one of the chests.

After he'd retrieved it, they sat together underneath.

Higher, the paraffin lamp hissed, guarding against the darkness that had spread itself over the world outside, as the remains of the rain dropped from the trees onto the roof of the shed. The storm had passed. The thunder sounded as far away as the morning.

Winnie bent her head against Cob's shoulder.

They warmed each other.

"I'm afraid of what's out there," she said after a quiet while. "Let's stay like this a bit longer."

Their warmth grew deeper, eliciting sleep.

"My grandfather played the acoustic…" she said.

"Guitar…" she said.

"I like it here," she said.

"I'm glad…" she said. But, before she could finish, sleep slipped past the flickering light and stole her thoughtlessly away.

Winnie awoke in the shed, wrapped snugly in the blanket. Cob was gone. The paraffin lamp was gone. The air was cool. A bundle of clothes sat by the door. She dressed and stepped outside. The sky was overcast. The world was colourless and mute. She trudged toward home through the remnants of last night's rain showers. She brought the blanket with her. "Cob," she said, walking through the door. But there was no answer. She said the same into every room, and every room did not answer. She sat on her bed and hugged her knees and saw that the backs of her ankles were still sore. She rubbed them and was glad that at least she had this temporary reminder of the colour the winds had blown into her life, even if only once and for only a few hours. Life persists, she told herself as she ate breakfast, and remembered the jars she had left with Arnold. She would have to get them. Maybe Arnold would decide to buy a few more. She put on her homemade boots. She left the house, turned toward Black Bear Portage, and there it was:

Cob's guitar!

Her heart leapt and she called out his name.

But, again, there was no answer.

Her heart fell.

But it did not fall completely, for somewhere deep within her soul (if such a thing exists) she felt the twinkling of a fledgling, strange sensation. She couldn't name it. Indeed, she'd hadn't experienced it before. But she knew that it was real. She couldn't explain — or even understand — how she knew that, but she did. It was a certainty. Just keep the guitar safe and wait. Just do that and *Cob will come back, because the guitar is the most important detail.*

She closed her eyes and pictured their reunion.

Her lips twitched.

For an instant, the picture of the imagined reunion twitched with them — a barely perceptible distortion. For an instant, Winnie wasn't sure whether this new sensation was a blessing or the first symptom of some terrible disease.

But then she smiled.

And the distortion disappeared.

And the Midnight Trio

◆◆◆◆

by Harper Eliot

And the Midnight Trio

The radio buzzed and crackled into the low-lit room. It struggled there, ten feet underground, pressed against the cold brick wall, searching for radio waves with its coat hanger aerial. Sometimes it gave up altogether, hissing and sputtering out, begging to be switched off at the outlet. One of these days it wouldn't turn on again. But Violet hadn't bought the radio; it wasn't hers. It was an unrequested luxury, and the idea that it was her job to replace it, or even that it required replacing, hadn't crossed her mind. It had been there before her.

Frowning, she leaned a little closer and listened, trying to hear the muffled song through the crowding static. She felt the disappointment bubble in her seconds before she identified the song as another manufactured pop hit sung by an auto-tuned peroxide blonde, and she switched the radio off.

Stretching her arms above her head she felt her shoulder crack and the muscles in her back tense below her ribs. She wondered when the crack had started. She'd noticed it one afternoon last week, brushing her teeth in the dingy shower at home. Or perhaps it was two weeks now. The days had begun to bleed into one another, running on into hours and seconds. Sometimes she looked at the clock above the cooker in her kitchen and couldn't decipher the hour by the thin arms. Insomnia had something to do with that. But Sunday, Sunday stood as a marker. Solid, unmoving, restful Sunday. The club was closed, and she always knew it was Sunday because Sam would be in her bed, snoring softly against her cheek.

Maybe that's tomorrow, she thought as she lined her eyes in thick black. She stood, bent over her dressing table, her face close to the mirror, trying to judge colour and detail in the ever-dimming light. One of these days she would remember to bring the white Christmas lights from home and string them up around the table. For now she let her memory-imprinted hands blindly paint her face, and hoped for the best.

Time had become elusive when Violet started working at the club; that much she knew. It was being nocturnal, and it was the suggestive nature of nightlife. She had also noted that as time became less present, she had to work harder to keep her cares in line with the cares of her employer. David was nice enough; thoughtful, reasonable, funny, kind. But he wasn't going to let her get away with being less than she had been when she auditioned. Every night, when she arrived at the club, she would work hard to remember her fresh-faced enthusiasm, and attempt to replicate it in the mirror. Some nights she slipped; but with concentration she could still paint ambition on her lips.

Violet used to pretend she had been hired for her voice. It was steady and strong, beginning to balance between liquor and smoke, finding the rich notes and the husky breath.

It was pleasing enough, and she knew how to put it to use, but more recently she didn't mind telling herself the truth. She had been hired because she knew how to flirt. Not just with coy smiles and witty comebacks, but with the turn of her wrist and the angle of her hip. She knew how to sell sex without stripping or even licking her lips. She could press her ear to her shoulder and send shivers through her audience. One night she had hovered her spiked heel over the wire of her microphone and watched the club's patrons squirm and lean closer. Another night she had crouched at the side of the stage eating an apple, watching the rest of the band tap and strum laconically through a beautiful instrumental piece. The folded shape of her legs beneath her, steady and compact, had been enough to play into the audience's hands. She had been offered a lot of cocktails after the set that night.

"I was going to give you a warning for that," David told her later as they shared a bottle of wine on the roof. "That was piss-poor showmanship. But the bar took about £200 more than usual. Keep it up."

Maybe there was even an art to seducing money out of rich businessmen, although she doubted the painters down the road at St. Martin's would agree. Nevertheless, David was pleased and Violet received a fair share of the takings considering she only worked two hours a day. Sam said she needed another job. She could survive on the money she earned at the club, but he said she deserved more than that. She shouldn't work the bare minimum and spend her remaining twenty-two hours at home waiting to go to work.

"Don't you want to do something during the day?" He asked, lacing his fingers through her hair.

At the time she had frowned, hungover. It had been a long time since she had woken up feeling capable of doing anything during the day. The hours between sleep and work were for recovery. On Sunday night, neither drunk nor working, she had thought about it again. It couldn't hurt to take better care of herself. Fewer cigarettes. Less alcohol. Her sister and her brother-in-law were always detoxing in January. Violet had scoffed at the thought, but couldn't help admire the glowing, even tone of her sister's skin when they gathered for their father's mid-March birthday.

But even with her sister standing as evidence for potential improvement, and after Violet's resolve at the end of the weekend to take better care of herself, by Monday she was rationalising it away; what had she ever wanted with sobriety? She liked alcohol because it was engaging. It filled hours she had never been able to fill before.

Still, the thought was there. In an attempt to get her to take an interest in his subject — she forgot now what it was — a teacher at school had told her that interest was the first symptom of love.

Looking at her reflection she murmured to herself, "One day I'll take an interest in something and it'll be worth being sober for."

For now she was content flirting with the *concept* of 'taking an interest'. Tonight she was a star — young, with a lust for flesh to tease, and substances that you could only buy under the counter. Neither of these were a problem. She never had anything more than hangovers to worry about. Besides, she could still stand on the stage, professional and talented, and look down her nose at the wasters on the street with red track marks on their forearms. She was nothing like them.

She was distracted from her reflection by a knock. Sam stepped into the room, his sandy hair tousled, only half dry after his late and rushed shower. Despite his haphazard approach to maintaining a professional appearance, Sam always looked well turned-out. His white shirt was crisp, and under the stage lights his hair would fall softly over his brow before they even started playing.

Walking over to her as she pressed her rouged lips together, he slipped a calloused, possessive hand around her waist, stroking the pale, naked flesh of her concave belly.

"What time is it?" She asked, setting the gnarled lipstick down on the surface of her dressing table.

"We have time." Sam pulled her slender, boyish frame back against him and grazed her neck with his teeth. "Take your knickers off," he ordered as he snapped the clasp of her bra open and watched the lacy garment slip down her arms.

Once she had wriggled out of her plain white panties, he showed her his fingers, nails bitten down to the quick, before he put them inside her. It had been like this from the beginning. There had never been any question as to who called the shots. Sam took her as he wanted, and she let him because when they woke up in the morning he would grin and tickle her and show an interest in her wellbeing.

Unlike the patrons of the club, Sam seemed disinterested in the seductive flex of her shoulders. He had kissed her, that first time, standing on Waterloo Bridge after she had spat into the water below. With his teeth in her lip he had hissed at her not to "fucking spit in the Thames". She'd laughed and he'd planted a death grip on her neck and walked her, like that, all the way back to his flat.

As he drew the slickness from her willing cunt with his masterful fingers, Violet felt herself, ten years younger, fawning over musicians with her adolescent obsessiveness. Like all the girls her age she had kissed posters of boy-bands with her shiny, pink, glossed lips, leaving them sticky and adored. Of course, it was different with Sam; he was neither fawned over nor pretty. He didn't possess the requisite chiseled jawline for teenage fandom, and his body was more tense than toned. But his smile was genuine, unashamedly showing the overlap in his front teeth, and when he pressed his deft fingertips between her thighs, she felt the skill of a musician, in control, in charge. He worked her body, pressing dimples into her flesh, and leaving purple bruises when she let him.

Their eyes met as he cupped her breast in his other hand, still grazing his teeth into the hollow above her collarbone. His reflection was of a man, unkind, uncaring. Violet gasped to think how others would see him; so cruel. They wouldn't know the purring smiles she awoke to, nor how her body sang as he bit into her flesh.

He had drawn blood once.

Feeling her cunt give way under his touch, flooding his fingers, he slipped one hand to her neck, unbuttoning his trousers with the other, and pushed her down, over the table. There was something skilled but mechanical about how he knew and used her body. Still she moaned in ecstasy as he drew scratch lines down her back, and slipped himself inside her.

As he thrust into her, deep and self-assured, he ran his fingers between the purple butterflies inked just under her skin. Three points of colour on her pale flesh. She flexed her muscles just so and he could swear he saw their wings flutter, pulsing against her heartbeat.

The butterflies were the work of Sam's friend, India. For the first one, Violet had lain on Sam's bed, on her stomach as India straddled her waist and seared her skin with the needle. At eye level with Sam's belt, Violet had watched him grow hard while she winced and fought to remain still. He had placed his firm hands on her shoulders and Violet had wondered if it was to keep her still, or to satisfy his own lust for control. In either case, she buzzed between him and India, and when she was done, and India had left, she let him touch the marks, making her moan until he was hard enough to fuck her.

Now, with her breasts pressed into the wooden dressing table, Sam drove himself into her again and again. She could hear where they met, their bodies forced together with each penetration, and although aroused, she knew he was taking her for his pleasure, and that he would be done long before she found any satisfaction.

Gasping for breath, her ribs forced hard into the wood, Violet strained to look up, into the mirror, to see the mask across her lover's face. He grunted, his gaze hungrily fixed on the sight of his cock pushing her open. Turning her head a little further, she felt her neck ache and stretch.

"I love you," She gasped.

Reaching out, he slapped her cheek hard and growled as he began to cum, filling her cunt, spurt after spurt. She felt it, thick and sticky, coating her insides. She could feel her cheek burning, but she grinned anyway, blissful at the way he fucked her.

Stumbling back, breathing hard, he withdrew and moved to lean on the arm of the sofa. Violet stood up, feeling his cum leak out of her. She reached down to pick up her knickers, but he cut his hand sharply through the air to stop her.

Catching his breath he spoke. "No underwear."

Peering out into the audience from between the worn red curtains Violet decided it must be either a Friday or a Saturday. Whilst the club was popular, it was never quite this full during the week. She hoped it was Saturday, as she could feel the weight of tiredness in her feet, and their frenzied fucking downstairs had made her hungry for Sam.

She longed to take him home with her and keep him tucked under the duvet on her unmade bed.

Standing in the wings, Sam kept one firm hand on Violet's hip as they watched David tread the stage, welcoming everyone to the club that night. Violet tried to listen for some mention of the day of the week, but if David said it, she missed it. Maybe it was when Sam leaned in to whisper in her ear, giving her unusual comments that had become regular between them.

He cleared his throat. "And don't look for me after the set. The guys and I are going over to Gordon's to play there. I'll be back about midnight."

Violet nodded that she understood and wondered, again, what time it was.

"Anyway, enough about me!" David grinned, ever friendly with his audience as they chuckled in response to a joke Violet hadn't heard. Although not a compère by trade, David was confident and just funny enough to fill in time between acts — or Violet assumed he was. Truth be told she had neither the attention span nor the inclination to listen to him any more. She frowned in the wings, running lyrics through her head like facts memorised for an exam and trying to ignore how Sam's hand grew tighter on her hip. Eventually she was awoken from her reverie as David gave them their final introduction. "Please welcome our house band, Violet and the Midnight Trio."

A warm smile from Sam as he walked out into the lights, and Violet followed after the other musicians.

The audience, slightly drunk and very lethargic, gave a light but appreciative round of applause as the band took their places and the first song started. Violet sank into the music, feeling the tinkle of the piano, a tap on the high hat, and Sam's low thrumming bass carry her forward until it was time for her to open her mouth and sing.

Standing there, singing songs she knew as well as she knew her own face in the mirror, she was brought to a different kind of consciousness. Onstage she always noticed how her thoughts became larger as her body was busy. Hitting that first high note, she raised her hand to her face, wrist bent to accent the sharp line of her jaw, and came, more fully, to terms with the reasons behind her employment. After all, no matter how much she loved singing, she was never as aware of the notes that parted her lips as she was of the eyes that searched her angular, boyish body for feminine reflexes.

Refused the luxury of underwear, Violet had slipped into a blue silk dress that slinked around her body, creating the illusion of curves as the light played over its sheen. It worked well enough that no one noticed the slightly frayed hem or the small tear under her arm. Stage lights were, for the most part, unforgiving, but the distance between her and the audience hid such slight sins.

Alive with the music, Violet was awake. She never realised the half-conscious state she lived her life in until she was performing; and as soon as the performance was over, she would forget. But for now she was wide-eyed and aware of every flicker of movement in the room. In particular, the way the gentleman to the left of the stage shifted in his seat, dipping his hand briefly below the table from time to time. Just some minor discomfort, almost certainly, but Violet felt the thrill of being wanted bristle across her skin.

The first night she had sung at the club, the wanton eyes of her audience had come as a surprise. All the nerves she had held in the wings about remembering the notes and annunciating the words dissipated as she became minutely aware of her body. Every inch of skin pulsed with uncertainty as she tried to seduce her audience and trick them into hearing something better than she could produce. It was a while before she found her rhythm, but that first week she was carried on the advantage of being a novelty. It didn't take long for her to identify herself in their eyes. For the suits and gentlemen, this club was one step below burlesque and striptease, and for a month or so she was the new girl at the harem, wanted and paid for handsomely.

Violet had mourned the novelty as it wore off, but found comfort in cementing herself as a coy seductress. She might have lost her initial appeal, which held so much excitement, but at least she was in control and as far as she could tell, or as deep as she imagined, still wanted by the majority.

Turning to show the room her naked back and entrance them with the purple butterflies, she glanced at Sam. Head down, fingers curled around his instrument, he played with intense concentration, barely present on the stage at all. All movement was between him and the double-bass, his first love. Violet didn't mind playing second to the grand, dark instrument, and had sometimes felt honoured as his deft fingers thrummed across her body, deepening the heaving of her chest as he pressed between her labia.

The song was sad, but nowadays, when she sang it, she saw it more as cogs and wheels, intricately interconnected, creating something larger than the sum of its parts. It no longer inspired awe in her, but she enjoyed listening as they performed, lulled on the way the piano fit so perfectly with the rhythm of the drum, and steadfast in her participation, crooning high melodies above their solid foundation.

During those first few weeks, singing night after night, it was not just learning how to flirt that occupied her mind. Each night, up on stage, she would listen to the incredible music made by the three men behind her, and after every set she would hide to avoid being fired. Sam and his friends were experienced, talented musicians. They had been playing together professionally for seven years. Seven years earlier, Violet had still been at school. Now she was waiting to be found out; waiting for David to spot that she was a fraud, and throw her out by the back door.

Once secure in her position, and with enough encouragement behind her to let her know she wasn't in danger, it became harder for her to pretend her youth wasn't a commodity. David was selling her age, and, she later discovered, at quite a profit. She could have hit flat notes every night and he wouldn't have fired her. A girl who could still put on a pleated skirt and pretend to be virginal, sweet sixteen was by far the greatest selling point the bar had. But simultaneously, his respect and patience were not things that could be earned with money. Violet sought to live up to her audition, because to be great in David's eyes was something to aspire to. He knew people, and wouldn't suggest anyone without talent, no matter how pretty or virginal she was.

Violet had subtly grown up, but she never hid her age from view. She always let her giggly smile show at some point during the set, and she often came out to the bar after the show and let the patrons buy her drinks, getting a closer look at her unlined face. It was a compromise everyone seemed satisfied with.

Tonight, a few tables back from the stage, in the middle of the room, sat two businessmen. One was Sam's age, with brown-red hair and a chin dusted with stubble. He was broad in his shoulders and easily distracted by the waitresses, his eyes glittering across their lithe bodies. But he caught Violet's eye because she caught his. She spotted him there because, as he watched her sing, his expression became dreamy and his eyes grew wider, shining in the dimly lit room. She played with him, licking her lips between phrases and arching towards him. His expression, when she handed him these glimmers of hope, was wishful, his pink lips an open grin. But he was still distracted, from time to time, by the women milling through the audience, balancing glasses on trays too heavy for them, and as he looked away, breaking eye contact, Violet had found her gaze playing across the figure of his companion at the table. Far more enigmatic, the other gentleman was older, perhaps by twenty years, and Violet soon noted that his eyes never left her figure. But his expression was neither displeased nor lascivious. He watched her carefully, as though she were the object of an experiment he was observing. It both thrilled and unnerved her. This kind of attention was not unheard of, but he seemed particularly good at veiling his thoughts.

He must be in charge of something, she thought as she watched his self-control. He could have been silently damning her for her sins. But he could just as easily have been imagining the feel of her silken thighs beneath his palm.

As she caught the edge of that thought, Violet felt the heat of her cunt between her legs, a tiny tingle that sparked up into her abdomen. She clasped the idea between her fingers, and let it course through her body as she sang.

The rest of the set became a performance for these two men, not so much for their benefit, but for her indulgence. As she played to their movements and whims — bending her leg slightly if she saw a pair of eyes drop to her thigh, or tousling her own hair if one met her gaze — the desire she felt coming from them fed her ego and her arousal. Her breaths became panting, breaking hazy phrases of song as her skin grew slick beneath her clammy palms. Arching under the stage lights, all sensation coursed into her heated cunt, until she could feel the wet warmth pulsing between her thighs. She moved to relieve the pressure, to assimilate some semblance of propriety and professionalism, but whenever she opened her eyes and raised her gaze, she was met by their expressions.

By the time the final notes played, she was heady with narcissism, swimming on a wave of immodesty. As they left the stage, Sam slipped between the curtains with her and kissed her cheek roughly.

"Nicely done. We're off. Get yourself a drink; it's hot under those lights."

With that, he disappeared. His staccato run of small orders jarred into her mellifluous buzz, but she liked it. She enjoyed the way he punctuated her consciousness, keeping her awake.

David was back onstage, welcoming the next band. Sam and Violet were just filler at the club; later sets were reserved for hired acts, for names. Violet put this out of mind as she slipped round the wings and stepped out into the club, heading towards the bar. She preferred to pretend she was the star.

Fred was working tonight. Fred looked more like a bouncer than a barman, but he was charming and his thuggish appearance put the patrons at ease: it seemed unlikely that any girls would go home with Fred rather than the suave, money-drenched businessmen who affected so much cosmopolitan sophistication. In actual fact, many of the patrons were slimy up close. Once, in her early days at the club, Violet had gone home with Fred. He was a little clumsy, but he gave himself completely to passion and fucked her hard as she dug her nails into his wide back. In true clichéd style they had lain side by side afterwards, smoking cigarettes and staring at the ceiling. Although the sex itself had been more than satisfactory, what she liked most about it was how easily they slipped back into being friends, both aware that it had been good, but that they probably wouldn't do it again. In the real world they didn't quite fit. Besides which, Violet had fallen into Sam's bed shortly afterwards.

Fred made his way towards her, grinning warmly. "Hey sweetie, nice set. Usual?"

"Please."

Fred poured her a gin and tonic, adding a little more gin than is customary, and Violet took it, immediately drinking deeply through the crooked black straw. She finished it fast and ordered another.

As she turned back to the audience, leaning on the granite surface of the bar, she spotted the two businessmen, walking in her direction. Now standing, she was pleased to note that both men were over six feet tall, towering above her as they reached the bar and casually ordered. Fred flashed her a warning look as she glanced over her shoulder, but grinned as he retrieved a bottle of red wine from beneath the bar. As he rang up their bill and the older man paid, the younger man shamelessly ran his eyes across her body.

Up close Violet could see all the flaws in his skin; the rough stubble, the marks and scars — perhaps the remnants of adolescent acne. She observed him carefully, immediately romanticising his imperfections. If he had been the weedy, nerdy boy at school, there was success in his presence and confidence now. In looking her up and down, he held up his middle finger to all the bullies and snide remarks in his school days. She didn't ask, but in her imagination she could see his entire education, how he grew up, and the girl at university — maybe even Oxford or Cambridge — who slipped into his bed with him. He had filled her with cum and her burning eyes had taught him self-assurance. She would have had to be beautiful, and not self-doubting. Perhaps an amazonian brunette, with a full smile and thick, glossy hair. All of it, of course, had led up to this moment, standing at the bar, filled with confidence, preparing to approach Violet.

"You were great up there." He interrupted her reverie, tilting his head towards the stage.

Releasing her bottom lip from the thoughtful grasp of her teeth, she regarded him evenly. "Thank you."

"What did I tell you?" The older man didn't look up, busy pouring wine into two elegant glasses. "She's always great."

Turning her attention to him she thought, perhaps, she had seen him before, half hidden in the shadows of the room, watching her perform. There were a few like this — rich, observant, who kept themselves back for fear of being observed.

"This is Liam," the older man explained, introducing his companion.

Violet granted Liam a little smile. "Hey Liam." Her voice lingered a moment on the minuscule rise and fall of his name.

"Liam's very competitive. Knows what he wants."

Violet felt a tiny frown crease her brow, but she remained quiet, casting a bemused glance at Liam, who was grinning incredulously at the older man.

"Well, go on then." The older man looked expectantly at Violet as he passed a glass to Liam. The moment his eyes settled upon her Violet could feel the weight of expectancy. She shifted uncomfortably.

Unsure what he wished her to go on with, Violet maintained an expression of good humour and shook her head lightly. "No, no, please, you."

"He's handsome, don't you think?" The older man addressed Violet directly, his expression unwavering, unreadable.

"Okay, thanks John. We get the picture," Liam cut in, laughing off the compliment. "I'm sorry. He likes to be in control. My boss, you know."

Violet raised her chin in agreement. "I know the feeling. Someone else in control." Liam and John simultaneously swept her body with their eyes and returned to look into her face. "So what's your business? What do you do?"

"Oh, it's very dull," John said dismissively, waving the thought away. "We're in advertising. The money side."

"Does that mean you're rich?"

John laughed, a warm chuckle that rose in his throat and spread across his lined face. Within arm's reach, Violet decided that her assessment of him was correct. He was at least fifty, possessing the kind of self-knowing contentment that comes with age. Compared with his lithe, toned companion, John was a little thicker around the waist and neck. But this only served to cement him, in her mind, as an unmoving powerhouse, a quality that was growing ever more attractive as she looked between the two men.

"It means I'm rich. It means that, if he plays his cards right, Liam will be rich," John nodded, his expression still warm and amused.

"What do you do for him, Liam?" Violet sipped from her drink, the straw caught between her teeth.

"I'm an apprentice. You could say I'm learning how to be him," Liam glanced at John, as if to check that he was correct.

"And that's what you want, is it? To be him?"

It was Liam's turn to laugh. "Well, you know, I…." He broke off and started again. "Of course. Who wouldn't? John's a big deal, you know."

She nodded. The room broke into a light round of applause and their attention turned, briefly to the stage. The singer, a blonde woman with an hourglass figure clad in rich red, bowed her head lightly in thanks before the next song began to play.

"What did you tell him about me?" Violet asked, curiosity getting the better of her cool demeanour.

"That there was a beautiful, boyish girl who sang sultry, seductive songs in the heart of Soho."

Liam took a sip of his wine, watching Violet over the curve of his glass. "He was right."

The unmoving weight of their attention pressed into Violet as she crossed her left arm over her body and clasped her naked shoulder, massaging it lightly with her fingertips. It ached deeply where it had cracked earlier, coursing hot lines of pain down her back as she arched her spine lightly.

"Are you okay?" Liam seemed concerned.

"Just an ache," Violet turned to show him her shoulder and her naked back. "Just here."

John cleared his throat, the grating noise catching Violet mid-pose. "We were going to find a booth. Would you like to have a drink with us?"

She nodded carefully and they made their way to the back of the club. The booths were all taken, overflowing with suits and girls in expensive dresses. At one end, a jocund group of young men lifted their beer bottles to toast a young, blonde-haired man. A stag party, Violet guessed. In another booth, a short, dark haired man bristled lasciviously against the body of a demure brunette. Violet had seen her here before, with other men, and been introduced to her in a nearby bar once. A prostitute. High class, of course. After their introduction Violet had lain awake all night, wondering if she would ever fuck for money. It was in her early days singing at the club, when life seemed a little unsure. She hadn't found her allure yet and was waiting, day by day, to be fired. *And if I am,* she thought, *I wouldn't want to give up my flat.* A girl's got to eat.

"Nothing free," Liam frowned, looking around once more.

Feeling the buzz of the gin in her veins, Violet looked at the back of John's neck, where his hair was neatly cropped, and liked the attention he gave to his own detail. "I have somewhere we can go," she said.

Balancing on the chair, Violet leaned over her dressing table to flick the radio on. It crackled awake and piped something audible into the room. It would do, she decided, to negate any awkward silence. Behind her, John and Liam sat comfortably on the frayed, blue velvet sofa, pouring more wine. Having not yet decided what her intention in bringing the two men to her dressing room was, Violet hovered over the radio for a moment, downing her third gin and tonic. As the nighttime DJs took over the station, the music became less recognisable, yet more atmospheric. It seemed to conjure up some sense of darkness and unease. Strangely, Violet felt more comfortable with it, as though labeling her own uncertainty helped her consider the situation. For a few minutes she waited, wondering if perhaps it was close to the hour, hoping the DJ might give her some indication of the time.

One song came to an end and another started, timeless and endless and finally, slipping from the chair, she turned to smile at her two companions, one hand resting on the dressing table, her nails tapping the surface.

"Would you like some?" John asked, holding up the bottle.

She thought for a moment and nodded. All the stupid things she couldn't take back had, effectively, already been done. At least alcohol would lubricate whatever happened next. Taking up the empty teacup that stood in amongst her make-up and jewelry, she walked across the room and held it out for John to fill.

They drank in relative silence, only exchanging the briefest of remarks as the evening wore on, the radio filling the space with white noise.

Draining his glass, John set it down on the floor and sat back, his fingers splayed across his knees. He looked up at Violet as though she were a piece of artwork being assessed for value. He nodded briefly.

"How's the shoulder?"

Violet raised her hand to touch her bare skin. "A little sore."

"Liam can help you with that." He turned to his young apprentice who quickly swallowed the wine he was sipping and put down his glass.

Placing his hand on the sofa between the two men, Liam beckoned Violet with a gentle tilt of his chin. "If you'd like."

There was something about the angle of his wrist that put her in mind of her first boyfriend. Boyishly clumsy, he had been confident enough to make the first moves. At the tender age of fifteen — or maybe fourteen, or thirteen — they had sat on the wall outside a dying party, sharing a bottle of cheap beer, and he'd slid his hand across her lap, warm and firm with drunkenness, kissing her waiting lips.

Violet took her place between the two men, settling on the edge of the sofa as Liam's hand came to rest on her back, slipping the thin strap of blue silk over her shoulder and letting it fall a little way down her upper arm. His thumb explored the shape of her muscles, seeking the knots and easing them out into her soft flesh. Breathing deeply Violet allowed herself to relax into his knowing fingers.

His touch was full of promise and electricity and, as he massaged the small spot, releasing the burning pains that had shot into her chest throughout her set, Violet half held her breath, waiting for him to explore further, across the expanse of her naked back. It didn't take long. Soon he was smoothing her skin, skating his fingertips over the butterflies, tentatively moving to her lower back and inside the silken material of her dress. She girlishly wondered if he could see the tear under her arm, where the material was slightly darker, and if he would mind the frayed hem if she was out with him properly.

As he reached the angular shape of her hip, he kissed her shoulder, pausing there to let her feel the rough stubble on his chin.

It was moments like these, always moments like these, that allowed Violet to escape the mundanity of day to day life. She wasn't sure when exactly she had agreed to sit and live with boredom, but she went to sleep each night with the wish that she was living a more extraordinary life. Meanwhile she made no attempt to create any constant excitement, living instead off feelings such as these, the stubble of his chin grazing her milky flesh.

She liked the way his tongue darted from between his lips, so soft and wet, in stark comparison to the rough touch of his palms as they slipped around her waist, easily finding their way inside the loose, slinking material of her dress. He pressed his fingertips under the gentle curve of her lowest rib and she giggled at the suggestion of a tickle. She felt his mouth smile with her delight and one hand pressed down, towards the V of her upper thighs. Parting her legs a little, an invitation to his exploratory hands, she became more aware of herself, her body lighting up in hazy arousal. She could feel the minuscule movements of her dress against her breasts and felt her nipples harden as Liam put one hand, decisively, over her pubic mound.

The intimacy of his touch was heightened and exaggerated by the presence of John, sitting quietly to her left. As Liam slid his mouth against her shoulder and pressed his palm between her thighs, Violet looked at their voyeur questioningly.

John sat still, simply observing, his face neutral but with, perhaps, the hint of a smile as Liam reached up to slide the other strap from her shoulder, her dress falling about her waist and exposing her pink nipples to the cool air in the static room. Violet murmured her approval and Liam cupped one breast as his other hand pressed more firmly against her naked cunt.

Arching her back, she leaned into him, feeling his

middle finger slip between her labia, his thumb stroking the soft black pubic hair above her slit.

John leaned forward to see how she moved, how her nipples tightened with her arousal and protruded with her arched spine. But he didn't touch her, made no move to cup her untouched breast or smooth the skin around her naval. He simply watched as Liam's fingers pinched and bit her, saw how she sank into his hands and parted her wanton lips. John observed, and at the sight of his eyes, shamelessly exploring and skating over her nakedness, Violet felt her cunt grow wet, coating Liam's intrusive fingers.

She had never been watched like this, so close and explicit. No one had ever sat quietly to observe her in the throes of arousal. She had been seen before, accidentally or perhaps intentionally. She had heard the muffled giggles of tipsy teenagers who stole glances at parties as she tried to hide her activities behind half closed doors, wondering how far the gossip would spread by the time the school bell rang on Monday morning. But she had never been subject for someone's viewing pleasure.

Liam released her breast and pulled her back to lie across him, tugging at her dress and pushing it down her thighs until it pooled like oil at her feet. Naked between the two, who still sat in their suits, collars unbuttoned, but everything else intact, she felt like a plaything, orchestrated for their pleasure. Although she had been so brazen as to invite them down to her dressing room, it was John who had offered her to Liam. It was John who sat and took his passive pleasure as his apprentice used his hands to explore her body once more.

With her head against his chest, he placed one finger below her chin and raised her mouth to meet his. He kissed fiercely, as though taking as much as he could, devouring her lips and tongue, and his touch became more urgent. No longer stroking, he manipulated her limbs to accommodate him, all the while kissing her hard, biting her lips and teasing her teeth with the tip of his tongue.

Violet let a whimper escape, muffled by his lips, into the heavy room, and she felt Liam's body groan in response. Slipping her hands to his waistband, she unbuckled and unbuttoned him with deft fingers, until she held his heated erection in her palm, stroking him gently. He thrust up into her hand, his desire rough and commanding. She felt him pulse as she tightened her grip and the tip of his finger pushed inside her open cunt. Their gasps slowly fell into unison, their want synchronised and restless. Pulling her torso to face him and throwing her leg over his lap, he settled her astride him, her soaked cunt pressed against the base of his cock, the tip nestled against her pubic hair.

Looking into each other's eyes with delight, Violet made light work of his shirt, her fingers nimble as she unbuttoned him and opened the crisp white material over his chest, revealing lightly toned muscles and the softest smattering of hair.

"Perfect," John's voice broke their reverie and Violet, pressed against her heated lover, turned to look at the older man with heavy-lidded, lust-filled eyes. John sat back, one arm resting on the arm of the sofa, his face a little flushed but settled in an expression of comfortable amusement. Meeting her breathless gaze, he smiled. "Fuck him."

Violet bit her lip to stifle the growl that tickled her throat. His voiced commands conjured her basest arousal, and in her mind she saw Liam and herself, just bodies, twisted impossibly, fucking like animals, all carnality and passion, sweat and groans. Nothing beautiful, just taking their pleasure, in complete disregard.

Raising herself onto her knees, Violet placed her palms on Liam's chest and bit his mouth as he pushed his erection against her sex. She hovered there, teasing, not Liam, but John, who moved to see his apprentice enter her. But still she held back, rocking her hips gently against the tip of his cock, coating him delicately in her arousal. From where he sat, Violet knew that as she raised herself an inch higher, John could see the string of slick desire that stretched from her to Liam's cock. Watching John's eyes, Violet kissed the head of Liam's cock with her parted labia, again and again, thinking only of the older man, watching her tease. But beneath her, a strangled groan of frustration tore from Liam's throat and placing his hands on her shoulders, he drove her down onto him, engulfing his cock in one thrust, until she could feel his balls nestled against her buttocks. She gasped in surprise, as though she had forgotten him there, beneath her, a human being alight with need.

Now deeply penetrated, held tight, Violet pressed

downwards, grinding into his body, feeling him throb as she tightened around him and dug her nails into his chest. He yelped and reached to release her grip, taking her hands in his and moving inside her.

"No marks, little one," John said, his voice warm but authoritative. "Nothing he has to explain."

For the first time, looking down at their laced hands, Violet saw the gold band around Liam's finger, tight above his knuckle, and she felt a flicker of guilt cross her mind. But Liam's eyes were closed, his head back an inch as he raised his hips to penetrate her deeply, again and again.

As their movements deepened, speed increasing, Violet wondered how often John found girls for Liam to fuck. She wondered how many women had fingered the cold metal band as they rode his aching erection, or felt him slide between their thighs, all the while caught in John's binding stare. In her mind, Violet saw redheads and blondes and brunettes, on all fours, supine, pressed against a shower wall, fucked deeply, filled to gasping, the intimate wet noises slipping from between their bodies as Liam thrust inside them. She imagined the first night, John buying drinks and inviting a tall, willowy girl to their table, encouraging Liam's inquisitive, groping hands between her thighs and around her waist. Seducing her back to a hotel where John sat in an ornate, silk upholstered chair, and watched Liam crumble from a loving husband to a man driven purely by his desire to fuck.

Violet murmured something but found her words

stifled as Liam covered her mouth with his, and grasped her hips, lifting her, repeatedly and letting her sink back onto him. She moved with him, feeling her ass clench and release with each penetration, both breathless, her hands now gently tracing the shape of his stomach and chest.

She could feel Liam's blood heating under his skin as his pleasure built, his body tensing slowly, and she took control, moving a little slower. Liam's face contorted into frustration, and Violet kissed his lips gently.

"On the floor," John's voice was commanding once more and, looking at him, Violet saw the expression of a man in control, serious in his instruction.

With barely a moment for thought, Liam lifted Violet from his lap, and slid them both to the ground. Clasping his mouth to hers, she kissed him and made to lie on her back, his body over hers.

"No. Not like that. On all fours," came John's direction.

With one playful kiss, Liam leaned back to rest on his heels, his erection jutting upwards, glistening with the evidence of their activities. Slowly, deeply immersed in the languorous haze of sex, Violet turned and raised herself into all fours, parting her thighs to accommodate Liam's cock, which she could already feel pressed against her slit. From there, as Liam pushed inside her, Violet found herself looking up, directly before John, meeting his dark expression.

Liam's thrusts were ever more urgent, swift and deep, and Violet felt the impact of his movements ripple through her body, catching the edge of her panting breaths. She kept her dark eyes on John, watching him as he watched her. Like all the powerful men she had ever known, he sat with his knees apart, and she saw, or thought she saw, the swell of his cock between his legs as he leaned forward.

"Touch yourself. I want to see you cum."

Violet gasped, but whether it was due to the forcefulness of Liam's cock, pushing deep inside her, or surprise at John's words, she wasn't sure. Shifting her weight to one hand, she reached back with the other, under her tense body, and found the hard pebble of her clitoris. Teasing it with knowing fingers, she rubbed around the point, feeling the tingling pleasure in her cunt.

John moved further forward, and as Violet closed and opened her eyes, slowly, she watched him unbuckle his belt and reach into his groin to pull out his cock. Although short, it was thick and hard, a pearl of pre-cum glistening at the tip. He moved to position himself an inch away from her lips and began to stroke himself his hand slow, firm, certain.

Her fingers slipped faster across her clitoris and she felt the flush before orgasm creeping up her body, turning her cheeks pink. Nodding encouragement, John's eyes were like fire above her, his mouth open an inch and she could see the shine of his red tongue.

"Cum for me. I want to see you cum." He spoke low, his voice breathy, grating in the back of his throat.

The sensations from her own fingers and from Liam's relentless pounding built until she could feel herself balanced on the edge of orgasm. She gasped and panted, holding onto this moment, cresting the wave before the fall.

Her breath faltered and she pressed back, firmly into Liam. Slipping forward another inch, John pushed his cock against her parted lips and she came, opening her mouth to lick away his pre-cum, her body shuddering, her wrist growing weak beneath her as the climax ripped through her frame.

Dropping her hand to steady herself, she moaned around John's cock as he pushed in deeper. He wasn't rough or forceful, but smoothly in control, slipping his heated erection against her tongue as she gasped for breath. She felt the two men thrust and penetrate her in unison, John gently, pressing up against the roof her mouth, whilst Liam bucked his hips against her slick, hot cunt. She clenched around him, her body still wracked with the aftershocks of her orgasm, and he groaned loudly.

As they continued to fuck her, both taking their pleasure, she felt the ache in her wrists and in her knees, the carpet now too rough, and the ground beneath too hard. She felt her brow furrow as she sank deeper into the decadence of being fucked and feeling pain. She whimpered deep in her throat and John growled, the noises she made coursing through his dick and making him thrust a little more firmly. Grasping her head, his fingers lacing against her scalp, in her hair, John held her and thrust again, once, twice, and stilled, her nose pressed into his dark pubic hair, his balls against her lips.

A strangled noise came from John, his body tensing as he filled her mouth with his hot, sticky cum. She closed her eyes tightly, forcing her tongue to lick around the head of his cock as she swallowed, desperate to take every drop. At the sight of John releasing into her mouth, Liam arched his back and drove as deeply into her as possible. Groaning, his cum spilled around his cock.

For a moment, bodies softening, not one of the three moved. They all held their places and Violet's tongue slowed, the taste of cum coating her mouth as her back heaved.

Falling back on his knees, Liam slipped out of her and breathed loudly, through pursed lips. Placing his fingers around the base of his cock, John pulled out as well, releasing Violet's mouth and moving back to sit comfortably on the sofa as he buckled his belt.

Between them, Violet sank down to lie on her side, one arm beneath her head, the other crossed over her breasts.

"Whew," Liam laughed, feeling the tension leave the room, all three sated. His voice was breathy. "That was good."

"I knew she'd be good," John sipped his wine, speaking as though Violet wasn't there.

She felt the pulsing arousal of being used and discarded deep in her cunt and allowed her breathing to slow. The room still seemed full of intensity, and she noticed her nakedness more acutely now their bodies were disengaged, and pulled her thighs together. But she felt more subdued, their passionate noises no longer echoing on the stone walls, and became aware, once again, of the crackling radio. Raising her head for a moment, she strained to make out the lyrics of some half-obscured song.

Liam moved in front of her and leaned on one elbow. He traced the line of her cheekbone delicately. "You okay?"

She nodded, smiling weakly up at him.

"Good," He removed his hand and studied her face for a moment. "What's your name?"

Violet's eyes opened wide and she couldn't help but laugh. The fluttering amusement coursed from her stomach up into her throat, until she lay on the floor, giggling like a little girl. She heard John laugh quietly with her, and saw a crooked grin stretch Liam's mouth. No one spoke as the three laughed and Liam rolled onto his back, his hands over his face.

"Oh, man," He shook his head. "Sorry. Stupid question. What does it matter, eh?"

Violet smiled at him, unable to keep the pity from her eyes and patted his arm in a fraternal manner.

Breaking through the warmth of their laughter, the door creaked open and all three froze. Turning their heads, their eyes came to rest on Sam.

A little disheveled after working two shows in one evening, the autumn breeze had brought the pink to his cheeks. His face displayed no emotion whatsoever, and he stepped calmly into the room, closing the door behind him and setting his bag down on a chair.

Frowning a little he tilted his head to look at

Violet lying naked in the middle of her dressing room. She desperately tried to recall their conversation from earlier, trying to remember the time. He had said he would be back, had given her an hour. But his words escaped her.

"Shit," Liam scrambled to his feet. "Is that your boyfriend?"

Violet didn't speak, but just looked up at Sam with quiet adoration.

"Yeah, I am." Sam answered. "I think you guys had better go."

Liam quickly pulled his trousers up and grabbed his shirt, pulling it over his shoulders like a frightened rabbit. His eyes were wild, as he looked around to make sure he hadn't forgotten anything. John, in stark contrast to his jittery apprentice, stood calmly, collecting the wineglasses and the bottle, and left, nodding to Sam, Liam following close behind.

Alone with his girl, Sam reached across her dressing table and switched the crackling radio off.

Looking up at him, her eyes imploring, begging for forgiveness, Violet parted her lips gently. "I'm sorry."

Sam nodded evenly and made his way across the room to sit on the sofa. Spotting her teacup on the low side table, taken from her by Liam at some point in their frantic foreplay, Sam raised it to his lips and drained it. Placing it back down, he jutted his chin up, looking at Violet.

"Come here."

Raising herself up onto all fours she crawled to him and kneeling before him, placed her fingers in his lap. "I'm so sorry, Sammy, I'm so sorry."

Her eyes were wide and pleading but glinted not with remorse. Instead her expression bore excitement and expectancy. Playing his part perfectly Sam pushed her hands from his knees and patted the space on the sofa beside him. She climbed up, sitting on her heels facing him. He brought one hand up to stroke her cheek and she closed her eyes, nuzzling into his loving touch.

The moment quickly changed as he slipped his hand around her neck and pulled her down, roughly over his lap, her stomach flat against his thighs. Holding her in place, his hand firmly planted on her skin, fingering the hair at the nape of her neck, his other hand travelled down her lightly arched back and over the curve of her hip to rest on her buttock. Rubbing roughly, he dug his fingers into her pliant, white flesh.

"Bad little girl," He muttered under his breath as he raised his hand and brought it down, hard, on her exposed ass.

Violet's breath caught in her throat.

His hand came down again, faster, leaving a faint pink mark on her skin. Again and again. The rosy hue grew brighter, his movements quick and intense, blushing her skin until she was almost scarlet. She breathed heavily, turning to panting, sweat beading on her forehead as he spanked her.

The skin of his palm stung her flesh and she became aware, once again, of the ache in her wrists, and the light burn in her knees where she had been rubbed against the carpet.

A twinge in her neck reminded her of the angle John had held her head as he fucked her mouth, and further down, the familiar, bright pain in her shoulder, coursed along her spine, concentrated under Sam's violent hand. Gritting her teeth, her breaths sharp through her nose, she sank further into the decadence of the pain, hissing her whimpered response.

He held her in place perfectly, knew her body better than she knew it herself, and as he hit her and she screwed up her eyes, so close to her limit, so close to the precipice that would break, tipping the balance between pleasure and pain towards the latter, he slowed. She flinched under his delayed strikes and moaned, low in her throat. The broken rhythm set her on edge and she twitched at every missed beat.

Always, as he slowed, and she touched the edge of her consciousness, she remembered the first time, waking in the middle of the night to the image of his eyes glinting brightly in the dark, his hand exploring the curves of her bottom. She had given him the briefest of frowns, curiosity painting questions on her face. The stubble of his cheek brushed hers as he leaned forward and whispered in her ear that he wanted to put her over his knee. She had bristled, unsure of herself, but given into the young desire tightening in his body. That first time, she hadn't been sure. Curling against him afterwards, feeling her skin a little tender, he had brushed the hair from her brow and asked if she was okay. It took some getting used to. But now, she found herself thinking about it, wanting it. She sought ways to earn his palm. She displeased him and answered back, hungry for his admonishment.

Finally his hands loosened and calmed and he stroked her skin gently, bringing her back to the here and now. Her breathing slowed and she sank into his lap, tired, the burning in her skin much brighter now than when it began. As her focus melted from the pain in her buttocks, it moved out and she became aware of how slick she was between her thighs. There was, of course, the remnant of Liam, slipping from inside her, but with it, new heat.

"Violet?" Sam's voice was gentle and kind.

"Mm?" Her mouth would barely form words as he tickled her spine lightly, his other hand touching her bright red buttocks, pinching the raw skin.

"Did we agree on two?"

Violet opened her eyes and slowly moved to sit up, feeling his grasp loosen and release her. Looking at him, she leaned back, blushing, a little demure as she crossed her legs. "I...I don't know. They came as a pair." She watched him carefully.

Sam smiled at her. "I liked it. You looked used, there on the floor. More than usual. More than with one. More than usual." His voice trailed off, growing quieter as he thought, recalling the image of her, strewn across the floor, between the two men.

"You didn't mind?" Violet sucked her bottom lip.

"Mind?" Sam turned to face her properly, a small laugh bubbling in his throat. "No, sweetheart, I didn't mind. You looked beautiful. You know I like it. To find you. To see you like that." His eyes glinted playfully. "And to punish you for it."

"Even with two?"

Sam moved towards her, stalking up her body, kissing her stomach and her breast, her collarbone, her chin. "Two, three, four…as many as you like. And then I'll spank you and take you home."

Biting her neck, he moved up to take her mouth, pressing his lips against her and kissing her deeply. She let her fingers tangle in his hair as his tongue snaked past her teeth and found hers. She could feel the cotton of his shirt grazing her nipples as he moved above her, his body arched to cover her, his mouth devouring her. She pulled him close, let the rough denim of his jeans press against her wet cunt, still spilling cum as she pushed up into Sam's arms.

The city flew past in stark white lights and shuttered windows, and as the taxi turned to drive along the Thames, Violet could see the orange light-pollution of the city on the horizon, moving up through red and purple to show some semblance of darkness high above. She clasped Sam's hand firmly and he moved closer to her, pulling her against him as he kissed her neck, his tongue teasing that delicate space just behind her ear. Dissuading his tickling touch, she leaned her head against his shoulder and breathed in deeply, smelling the slightly salty sweat on his skin.

Just as her eyes fluttered closed, her body comfortable in the crook of Sam's arm, she felt his hand creep under her skirt and slowly up her thighs. She murmured something unintelligible, and he hushed her.

"I just want to touch what's mine, and feel it pool in my palm."

"What day is it tomorrow?" Her voice was no more than a murmur as she stretched her eyelids and glanced at the digital clock on the taxi's dashboard. 02.40.

"Sunday." He cupped his hand against her cunt.

She smiled into his jacket and fell asleep, feeling the warm pulse of his breathing in her hair.

Raw

◆◆◆◆

by Amélie Hope

Chapter One

Have you ever had a hunger awakened within you? A hunger so strong and full of fire that no matter how you try to rid yourself of the thoughts, it just doesn't go away? It sits there, somewhere in the dark recesses of your mind, playing its silent little tricks on you. On your body. It comes alive when you're asleep. It comes alive when you're awake. It swims around every inch of your mind until it consumes every part of your soul. You squirm and writhe in an attempt to rid yourself of its infuriating itch, but to no avail. It only burns brighter, a blue flame flickering with searing heat in front of your eyes until it's ready to explode throughout your entire being.

Hunger.

Need.

People look at me and think they know me; this sweet young thing, all smooth tanned skin, wide blue eyes, and long golden hair. The veritable all-American girl next door. Little do they know there is an animal within. I am a hunting tigress on the prowl for my next feed.

That's what brings me here tonight, to Damville Stadium. I am searching for my next meal. My next fix.

I can't sing. I can't dance. But I can get lost in the music. I *do* get lost in the music. It's my drug. Loud bass, screaming riffs, drum beats that vibrate their way through my body. Groupies. Drunks. Sex addicts. What can I say? I'm a junkie, getting high on the rock as well as the roll. It's my ecstasy. And right now I am in the midst of yet another high.

Looking up at the stage from my place in the front of the crowd, I fixate on the dude at the back; the guy who hides behind the drum kit, so lost in his set that the rest of the world disappears and there is only him and those beats. Josh. Last time he was in town he irked me, cornering me in the corridor of a bar where the band were hanging out. His grip on my arm was tight and painful as he dragged me passed the toilets and out into the derelict patio. He didn't need to speak to me, I knew what he wanted and I knew exactly how to give it to him.

Sinking to my knees on the grubby, cold stone floor, I unzipped his black ripped jeans, took out his cock and got to work, teasing him slowly, kissing the tip of his head before running my tongue along the length of his prick. I do so enjoy the tease, swirling my tongue around him before engulfing him completely, my throat now well trained to accommodate even the thickest of men.

It's so easy, getting these guys. They're all the same. So. Damn. Predictable. Ruled by their dicks. Even on the stage they're driven by the brain between their legs. Of course they don't do this for the love of the music, they do it for the love of the women. Or the men.

Josh, he likes men. Women *and* men. Usually together. Don't raise your eyebrows, it's pretty hot to watch. And be a part of. There is nothing more erotic than watching a beautiful woman sinking onto the lead singer of a rock band whilst he sucks furiously on his bandmate's cock.

The first time I saw this I was only nineteen. So young. So innocent. So pure. I was laying across a sofa in the dressing room of Solène, the female guitarist of *Hard Knocks*, a rock band from Brooklyn. We shared a bottle of vodka and giggled girlishly, chatting about anything and everything. Mainly sex. She pointed across the room and I turned to see a mass of limbs on the floor near the door, clothes shed and strewn haphazardly all over the place.

As I looked on, mesmerised by the threesome that was happening in front of me, I failed to notice the hands that cupped my breasts, caressing them gently through the black cotton of my vest. Or the lips that were kissing their way along the column of my neck.

"It looks hot, right?" Solène whispered against my ear in her thick Parisian accent, bringing me back to the present.

Realising for the first time what she was doing, I nodded mutely and looked down at the petite hands that gently kneaded my tits. Nineteen, virginal, watching group sex and being touched by a woman. An older woman. So I rose from the sofa and made a swift exit, right?

Wrong.

That was such a delicious introduction into the world of rock superstardom. A very delicious introduction indeed. And now, as I immerse myself in the music and the band on the stage, surrounded by thousands of men and women, sweaty and screaming song lyrics at the top of their lungs, I make a vow to get a repeat performance with that drummer. Only this time, it won't be me who's on bended knee on the cold stone floor sucking his cock. No, it will be he who has his face buried between my thighs, his tongue deep in my greedy little cunt.

"Get back here!" The security guard shouts as I run through the crowd, battling my way through the throng of gig goers.

I chuckle as the middle aged, overweight man attempts to catch up with me. Fool. I push my way towards the back of the stadium and out of the exit, wanting to make my move before the revellers start to leave. It's warm out tonight, the dark sky illuminated by tall festival lighting, and the air full of the smoky aroma of burger vans and hotdog vendors.

"Psst, Mattie!"

I turn to my left and see a lone female leaning casually against the metal railings that block the gig off from the public. My breasts tighten beneath the confines of my bra as I watch her place the slender cigarette in her mouth and take another long drag before blowing the smoke sensually from between her lips.

"Bibi!" I embrace her in a welcome hug. "It's been ages!"

"I know, anyone would think you've been avoiding me," she says with a wink. "I haven't heard a peep from you since Seattle and I know damn well you've been working the circuit."

I chuckle softly. Seattle — another amazing experience, my first date with another woman. An actual date. I met Bibi through Solène when I was twenty and we floated in similar circles, bumping into each other time and time again at different gigs and after parties. Three months ago, whilst *Hard Knocks* were playing an underground gig, Bibi had taken me by the hand and lead me into a world so new and fantastic that I had floated high on cloud nine for weeks after.

While Solène and the guys killed the stage that cool April eve, Bibi dressed me in a long black evening gown, took me to a high class cocktail bar, wined me, dined me, and then escorted me back to my hotel room, planting a sweet and unexpected goodnight kiss on my lips, which completely threw me and my bubble-fuzzy mind off kilter. The sweet goodnight kiss led to another, not-so-sweet passionate clinch, her tongue slipping between my lips and deep into my mouth, forceful and demanding.

I'd never made love with a woman before. Sure, I'd kissed and groped my fair share — Solène always delighted in petting my pussy until I climaxed around her fingers whenever we saw each other. But never had I spent the night alone with another femme. Bibi blew my mind that night, and she changed the way I viewed myself and my approach to sex. It wasn't just fucking to Bibi. She focused on sensuality; soft kisses, gentle caresses, tender touches. She nipped and nibbled her way across my flesh, never once demanding that I gave back to her. I was lost from the moment her lips pressed against my own. It was perfect. So perfect....

I slid the key card into my hotel door, grateful that it flickered green quickly, desperate to get my new friend inside. And then there was only us. Me and her. Two women who were about to experience each other for the first time. My heart pounded in my chest as she approached me, quiet and apprehensive about what I was about to do. This seemed so different to the other times; with Solène or other groupies. This seemed bigger somehow. More... meaningful.

Running her finger down my cheek, she gently coaxed me forth, leading me into the room and closely the door behind us. The first kiss was soft. So soft and so very sweet. Her lips were hesitant, but willing and I felt her melt into the kiss. Cupping my cheeks with her small palms, she drew me closer, deepening our kiss until I was completely lost. God...she was something else!

Unzipping the back of my dress, Bibi eased from garment from my body, letting the silky chiffon float to the floor as she stood back to admire the view. There I was, standing in the middle of my hotel room in a bra and panties, looking at her watching me. She reached out, smiling as she took my hand and led me to the bed.

We crawled onto the bed and knelt in front of each other, kissing again as I ran my hands down her sides. A blur of flying fabric and tangling limbs followed. She looked so fuckin' hot in that moment, as we lay together on the bed, naked and exploratory. I never knew this kind of sex existed; the tender kind. I thought it was all furious fucks and blowjobs. I never thought I'd meet another woman who would make me feel so alive, but as I palmed her large, heavy breasts in my hands I was high on the drug that was this woman. Beautiful Bibi.

I was slow with my movements, trying to ease myself into the night, not wanting to rush things or make some sort of rookie mistake. I mean, I had no idea what I was doing! I gently grazed my fingertips across her flesh, over her chest, down her arms, along her legs, and up to her clothed mound. Running a finger along the seam of her cunt, I was amazed at how wet she was. Wet for me.

A dark patch grew in the pale fabric of her panties as she became more and more aroused. I couldn't take it anymore, I had to touch her. Reaching out, I toyed with her cunt through her panties, teasing her flesh until I couldn't wait any longer. Easing the material from her body, I lay her down, wanting desperately to climb on top, to smash my body to hers and fuck her senseless. But she deserved more than a quick fizz-induced fumble by an overzealous girl who was still learning her way in the art of same sex relations.

I kissed my way down her body, moving from her lips, nipping her neck as I ventured south, eager to feel her breasts, to swallow her flesh and suckle on her teats. I pushed them together and lightly bit at her skin, lapping at her nipples before sucking harshly. Rubbing my cunt against her leg as I work, I lost the final vestiges of shame that fluttered around my mind. Could she feel how wet I was? Were my juices wetting her skin through my panties?

Leaving her breasts, I kissed my way down her tanned torso and settled between her thighs. Wow! She took my breath away. I've seen my fair share of naked women, but I had never seen anything as beautiful as her. She was so perfect, as if she's been carved from marble and come straight off the set of a porn film. But she was there and she was real and as I touched her soft lips, parting her with my thumbs, I was greeted with the finest meal I ever had.

She smelled divine, a hint of that wonderful womanly

aroma hitting my senses as I leaned in and kissed her there for the first time. I licked the length of her slit and smiled against her cunt as her juices spilled forth. I lapped at her, the cat that got the cream, drinking in as much of her as I could. Flicking my tongue over her clit, I felt it swell in my mouth, growing as I circled it slowly before sucking it between my lips. She gripped my hair, tugging at the strands as she writhed ad moaned. It appeared I was doing something right.

Pulling back, I slid a finger into her depths, amazed at how tight she was. She gripped me as I twisted and twirled, pushed and pulled against her inner walls. She was so warm, so…hot. I wanted for nothing but a cock of my own in that moment, to slide into her deeply and feel her slick running down my flesh. Without such an organ to command, I did the next best thing and fumbled in the low light for my favourite toy; a pink glass dildo. It was cool to the touch and feels fantastic against the most intimate of parts. I parted her labia gently and rested the tip of the cock at her entrance. I rubbed it over her flesh, across her clit, before bringing it to my lips and slipping it into my mouth. I sucked the hard phallus then brought it back to Bibi's cunt, pushing it into her inch by cool, glorious inch.

I fucked her slowly, flicking my finger across her clit, speeding up my movements in a desperate attempt to make her cum. I think she came, I'm not sure, but I no longer cared. I crawled along her body and kissed her again, pushing myself against her as I grew more confident. She cupped my mound through my panties and something inside me stirred. Her hand was warm and my pussy was thick with lust against her. She teased me, and I'm sure my sodden underwear surprised her, but fuck I was wet!

She'd never been intimate with me before, but she knew

exactly what to do...the way she touched me...teased me...tongued me, it was wonderful. She's *perfect. I don't know what I did to capture her attention, but I'm glad I did.*

"Earth to Mattie!" Her laughter brings me back to the present and I can't stop the blush that creeps across my cheeks.

"I'm sorry, I just, I...."

Sweeping my fringe across my forehead to get a better look into my eyes, she says, "No need for 'sorry' Matts, but now that you're here, how about a 'hello' kiss?"

I blush again, Bibi always has the power to render me speechless. As an independent and confident woman, it feels strange to grow suddenly shy as I always do when she's around. Glancing up at her through scruffy strands, I bite my lip and nod mutely.

Snaking one hand into my hair and the other around my waist, she pulls me into her body and I am instantly transported back to our night together all those weeks ago. I breathe deeply, inhaling her perfume and letting it wash over my body and into my panties. Her effect on me is amazing, my body hypersensitive and responsive to her touch.

"Please," I whisper and she grants me my wish, pressing her soft lips to mine in a lingering and lazy kiss.

She pulls away first, stroking my cheek lightly as she smiles down at me. "My dear, dear Mattie, so young and so very, very sexy."

I blush again, my cheeks flushing at her compliments.

I want nothing more than to grab her hand and lead her into the dark corners of the stadium, to pull down her panties and feast upon the silken cunt that I know lies within. Alas, I have other plans for tonight. Plans that may or may not involve Bibi.

"I said I'd meet Josh and Brandon in their dressing room when they came off stage," I say, trying not to let the lips at my neck distract me front the task at hand entirely.

"Mmmmmhmmmmmm," She murmurs into my skin before dragging her tongue across my flesh.

"Mmmmhmmm, wanna come with?" I ask breathlessly, all too quickly losing myself in the moment.

Pulling back, she grins at me with the look of someone who has mischievous plans of her own. "Thought you'd never ask. Lead the way, sexy legs!" She slaps my rear playfully and pushes me in the direction to which I was originally heading.

Chapter Two

We remain quiet as we meander through the corridors of the stadium, following the instructions Brandon gave me carefully, pausing every so often and making out brazenly to stop any disgruntled security guards from asking us too many questions.

"This way," I whisper, tugging on Bibi's hand and pulling her through the door to our left.

We stop short. Wow. This place is amazing. A dressing room with a difference. Usually they are barely comfortable, but this one is something else. No wonder the guys wanted to meet us here and not back at the motel. Bibi runs around the room like an excited schoolgirl.

"Look at this," she squeals, pushing her way through another door to the right of the room.

Joining her, we stumble to a halt in the doorway and stare in disbelief at the sight in front of us. Taylor, *Hard Knocks'* back-up guitarist, is sitting on the side of a hot tub, naked except for the ridiculously expensive-looking Gibson Acoustic that rests on his knee and covers his manhood. My breath hitches and my cunt clenches as I take in the scene. Two men in the tub in a passionate clinch as Taylor gently strums his guitar at the side, watching them intensely.

I look towards Bibi and see that she is just as captivated as me.

"I've never seen two men together before," she says quietly, her hand now holding mine, her thumb brushing my skin and causing a new wave of desire to roll through me. "It's so...so...so...."

"Hot?" I offer, not even trying to hide my arousal.

Turning towards us, Taylor smiles, his brown eyes gleaming as he notices our conjoined hands. "Matts, Bibi, Brandon said you might be joining us."

He stands and leans his guitar against the side of the tub. My clit swells as his erect cock brushes against my thigh while he kisses my cheek. I'm not sure whether I'm still high from the music out in the stadium or high from the sight of his fingers plucking the strings of his guitar only moments earlier, but I'm desperate to sink to my knees am take him into my mouth.

"Just as they told me," Taylor says as he draws the back of his hand across my cheek, "Such an angelic-faced slut."

"She's a gem, isn't she?" Bibi agrees as she pulls me into her and kisses my cheek. If she were a dog she may as well have pissed on my leg, marking her territory.

Taylor chuckles, "No fear, diva, I'm with them." He tosses his head in the direction of the men in the hot tub, neither of whom I've seen before. "Feel free to stay and enjoy the show!" With a wink he leaves us and slips into the water, joining the other guys for fun beneath the bubbles.

Bibi and I remain still and silent, watching the scene unfold with captivated intrigue. Who knew the sight of three hot tattooed rockers making out, stroking each other, prodding and probing, would be so hot!

"Bibi, you're here!" Solène squeals as she enters, running at her friend and embracing her tightly before kissing her square on the lips.

"Now *that's* what I call a hello!"

"I didn't think you'd actually come."

"As if I would miss your birthday, Sol," Bibi brushes her lips against her friends' and I wish that she was kissing me as she had done only moments earlier out in the corridors. Her lips are exquisite, a plump ruby red and soft as velvet. What I wouldn't give for just one more kiss.

Turning to me, Solène winks and grins slyly. "Now, I know it's not your birthday, babygirl, but I've got you a gift."

It's impossible not to fall in love with Solène, she's so vibrant and full of life, constantly throwing surprises in my face. At thirty-one, she's nine years older than me, but I've never had a friend like her. Best friends forever, isn't that what they say about those who can't seem to leave each other's side for longer than a day at a time? That's what Solène and I have become, addicted to each other, drawn together like moths to flames, like another drug, getting withdrawal symptoms. Sure, we've fucked a bunch of times, but we're more of a friendship with added extras thing.

Hopeless romantic that I am, I'm still holding out for Mr. Right. The search is looking bleak right now though. Fucking I'm great at, but finding a guy who will hang around for the pillow talk? No such luck.

"Mattie, may I introduce you to Nic," I follow her gaze as she turns towards the doorway.

Wow!

The world around me ceases to exist, the sounds of sex and chatter dissipating into background noise as I look at this man. Tall. Muscular. Ripped biceps bulge from the sleeves of his white t-shirt. His head is devoid of hair, but he sports a scruffy goatee and the expression that tells me he's as grumpy as sin. I like him already.

I extend my hand and smile, "Hi."

He regards me for a mere second before stalking passed and going to stand by the window.

"Isn't he divine?" Solène whispers excitedly into my ear as she starts to undress.

"He didn't even acknowledge me!"

"Sure he did, he looked at you didn't he? That's more attention than he gives most people."

I watch as she gets naked, marvelling at her figure and how she stays in such good shape. It must be all the sex.

"Come…watch me celebrate my birthday," She says excitedly and grabs my hand, pulling me into the bathroom where Bibi already now sits in the tub with the others, her large breasts bobbing in the bubbles.

Solène quickly joins them, three guys and two girls, all laughing as they begin to share their bodies for pleasure. I watch as Taylor hauls himself onto the edge of the Jacuzzi to allow his friend access to his cock, my own pussy moistening as he fucks himself into his friend's mouth. Solène moans loudly as Bibi grips her by her hair and smashes their lips together, their breasts rubbing together in the process. Usually I would be in there with them, but Nic…. Gorgeous, serious, solitary Nic has got me feeling all bashful.

Looking at Solène now, like this, so entangled in the web of lust with her friends I knew that she was where she was meant to be, surrounded by those who adored her and those who adored fucking her.

She really did have the sweetest of cunts, Solène. She taught me exactly how to kiss a woman on the nether lips in a way that was almost certain to induce climax on your subject. We spent hours practicing, with me, the good girl, on bended knee with my face buried between her thighs. Solène tastes divine, her silky nectar hinting at honey. I could feast on that pussy all day, had I nowhere else to be…other people to fuck.

Looking over at Nic in the far corner of the room I see him sipping from his beer whilst gazing out of the window. Odd. Wouldn't any red blooded male be watching Solène — who is now being spit-roasted in the middle of the floor by Josh and Brandon whilst the droplets of water drip off her skin — rather than looking the other way? Wouldn't he be lovingly stroking his big prick whilst Solène sucked furiously on Taylor's? Hmmmmmm. No, it would seem not.

"What can you see?" I ask quietly, following his line of sight through the pane of glass and into the industrial estate beyond.

"Eh?"

Ah, he speaks!

"Well, all I see are grey walls and corrugated iron roofs. It's not exactly exciting stuff." He looks back out of the window, perplexed by the conversation. "So, what do *you* see?"

He looks back to me, regarding me with deep green eyes as he takes another sip.

"I see two people, lovers, sharing a big canopy bed in the most amazing five star hotel in town. I see soft kisses, laughter, gentle caresses and an expensive bottle of champagne."

"Hmmmmm, you got all that from Mike's Motor Repairs? Not bad," I mused.

"I see you."

What?!

"What?!"

He holds out his hand and waits for me to slip my palm into his.

"I'm Nic, pleased to meet you."

I smile as he raises my hand to his lips and kisses it sweetly. Well what d'ya know, we have a gentleman in our midst. A very handsome, guitar strumming, tattooed hunk of a gentleman.

Chapter Three

Every so often you meet someone who takes you by surprise. Who makes you sit up and listen. Who makes your ears prick up, your eyes grow wide and your nipples tingle.

Every so often you meet someone whose lips you can't help but gaze at whilst he talks, mesmerised by the way she laughs. The way he smiles. The way he grows serious as you discuss the ways of the world.

Every so often you meet someone and secrets are shared. Desires expressed. Fantasies told openly as if talking about the weather.

Every so often you meet someone and it just feels easy. A friendship is born.

Every so often you meet someone and you know that even if you never see them again, you were still destined to share that smile.

I've only known him a week, but already I know that Nic is different to the others. There's something about him, the way he performs with such passion, that sets him apart from the rest. He's not on that stage for the fame, the money or the adoration from groupies. No, he's on that stage for one thing and one thing only — the love of music.

Watching him on the stage now as his band warms up for *Hard Knocks*, I can't help but feed off his energy, it radiates through the crowd, the whole place buzzing with musical electricity. He looks amazing, lost in his own world and his own thoughts; so focused on the music and that guitar. I'm mesmerised by his fingers and how they dance across the guitar strings making such beautiful sounds.

He scans the crowd for a long time before catching my eye, smiling and mouthing those special words every girl longs to hear: "I'm going to fuck you."

I blush, heat flowing into my pussy and cheeks with equal measure. Battling my way to the side of the stage, I have a brief altercation with security before managing to get backstage. Nic is standing with Brandon and Solène, laughing as they swig their beers, not caring about the sweat dripping from their flesh.

"Hey baby," he says, walking over, one arm sliding around my waist and drawing me close to him. I lick the sweat from his lips as he kisses me, revelling in the saltiness that leaves me craving more. The image of him naked flashes through my mind, dirty and hot from the stage, his strong hands gripping the back of my neck as he fucks my throat in the beautifully brutal way I love so much. Only he hasn't done that yet. Yes, we've taunted each other shamelessly. But no sex…yet. *God, I want him so much!*

"Take me home," I whisper in his ear, my sultry tone letting him know exactly what I want.

Nic looks at me for a moment, scrutinising me before slamming his beer down, grabbing my arm and leading me out of the room and towards his car. Once inside he leans over and kisses me forcefully before starting the engine and roaring away.

My heart is racing, excited with thoughts of things to come. No other moment has ever come close to this, to the nerves I feel now. The first time Brandon slid his prick down my throat and fucked it until I couldn't see through my tears, the first time Solène cuffed me to the bed so Taylor could fuck my tight cunt, the first time Bibi gently pushed me onto my back in the lavish hotel room and made love to me — all fall into distant memories as I sit in the car, adrenaline coursing through my veins as I think of touching Nic properly for the very first time. I attempt to control my breathing and the heaving of my chest by focusing on the dark road ahead, letting the bright streetlights wash dreams of pleasure through my mind. They cast a magical glow over the world at night and I hope desperately that this night is no exception.

The car rolls into the hotel parking lot a little too harshly and I turn to look at Nic. His face looks almost ghostlike in the dim light of night. My chest tightens at the thought of being with him.

"Let's go," he says and exists the car. I take a moment to compose myself and then step out of the car onto the gravel driveway.

Moisture pools in my panties as I follow him through the hotel lobby and into the elevator; that's a fantasy in itself right there! Nic opens the door to his room and heads straight to the kitchen area.

"This place is massive!" I exclaim, awed at how

palatial it is. A little too lavish for a guitarist in a rock band, perhaps? Fancy.

Nic grabs two glasses, filling them with vodka and ice. He hands me a glass, a smug grin on his face.

"Down in one?"

"Anyone would think you are trying to get an innocent girl drunk," I tease.

"Innocent? You are kidding me, right? Cheers!"

We clink glasses and I take a sip, looking at him nervously as he watches my lips caress the glass. Slamming his empty glass on the work surface, he grabs my waist and pulls me into him.

"Nic," I whisper, my mind too foggy to say anything else as he begins to nuzzle my neck.

"Mmm, you smell gooood,' he murmurs and nips my tender flesh before planting soft feather light kisses down my neck and along my collarbone. My eyes flutter shut, this man is driving me crazy.

"I want you, Mattie."

He kisses my neck softly then sinks his teeth into me, grinding my skin between his incisors. I am lost, mewing like a kitten who is being petted lovingly by her owner. His harsh nip speaks straight to my clit and I swell instantly.

Nic holds me to him so closely that I'm sure he can feel my hardened nipples grazing his chest. Suddenly, I'm up against the wall, slammed into the hard concrete by this eager mister. He's hungry, attacking me with fierce kisses that pin me in place with no room for escape. He's strong and heavy, pushing into me through layers of clothing. With my arms pinned over my head by a thick set of fingers to my wrist I am completely at his mercy. And there's nowhere else I would rather be.

Breaking the kiss first, he inhales deeply and stares into my eyes. I stare back. A challenge. A dare. Who will walk away first? Will anyone walk away or will we both see this play out to the bitter end? We remain like this for a long moment, a moment that seems to surpass time and go on forever.

The mood changes, no longer crazed and urgent. There is tenderness in Nic's eyes. He brings a hand to my face and gently strokes my cheek. My eyes flutter closed and I savour the touch of his fingers as they dance across my skin.

Uh oh, I think I've fallen for him.

My legs fail as he kisses me again, this time slow and heartfelt. Catching me as I begin to slide down the wall, Nic snakes an arms around my waist and holds me against him. Every touch, every kiss, every sound emitted from Nic's mouth mingles with mine and we are fused together in one ball of raw emotion. A lone tear escapes my eye without warning, suddenly overwhelmed by the situation unfolding before me. I don't do this, I don't do love. I do slut, dammit. Slut! I am losing control and it's scaring me.

Nic pulls back and takes my hands in his. "This is scaring you, isn't it?"

I look at the floor. I don't want to let my guard down, but I can feel the walls crumbling around me. I'm fighting so hard to keep him at bay but he is too powerful a force for me to reckon with.

"A little," I admit, feeling very shy and very vulnerable. "I don't usually end up in these situations."

Raising an eyebrow in disbelief, Nic laughs, "Oh c'mon now, I've heard all about the situations you end up in, Matts."

"Is that why you've brought me here? To get it on, then cast me out? To push me onto my knees and get my to beg for your cock like a good little lapdog? I thought this was different! Fuck. You."

For someone so large, you wouldn't expect Nic to be as gentle as he is. He doesn't get angry or rough, but simply takes my hands in his and silently leads me from the large, airy lounge through the hallway and up an ornate spiral staircase that leads to a big, soft-cream painted bathroom. I look around in awe; this place is amazing. In front of me on the opposite side of the room there is an enormous freestanding bathtub underneath a panel window. It's dark outside and the sky is dusted with thousands of stars glittering in the moonlight. The room is full of a balmy warmth that instantly sooths my soul. I turn to Nic and watch as he switches on the shower, the cubicle easily large enough to fit two people or more. I smile as he walks around the room, methodically lighting dozens of scented candles. Once they have all been lit he turns off the main lights and we are left there in the semi-darkness, the orange flames casting mystical shadows around the room. This is it.

Standing in front of me, he raises a hand and cups my cheek before leaning down to kiss me properly. This kiss is different to any other kiss that we've shared; it's not like the hungry one in the kitchen earlier, or the featherlike ones of the evening. This kiss is so much more. This kiss is a gift. Through this one kiss alone Nic is giving me his soul.

I open up to him, allowing his tongue to penetrate my mouth completely. It dances exotically over my own, tasting and exploring and in this moment I forget about everyone else. There is no Josh or Brandon, there's no Solène or Bibi, there's no Taylor or any other of the dozens of guys I've fucked over the last three years. There is only Nic.

In need of air, I pull away, giggling at the groan of disappointment he lets out.

"I'm not going anywhere," I whisper and stand back to admire him.

"That a promise, because there's something about you, Mattie."

"Something about me?"

He regards me closely for a moment and then responds, "Yeah. You're young and beautiful and a perfect little slut, but there's more. I can see it when I look into your eyes. You want more than the fucking don't you?"

I nod.

"You want the fucking, but you want the extra level of that 'something'. You want connection. You want love."

I nod again. I do want love.

"So," he says as he lifts my black vest slowly over my

head, "How about letting me love you?"

There's no bravado here. Nic doesn't need to whisper sweet nothings to get me to sleep with him, so why is he talking about love? A week after meeting and he wants to run off into the sunset.

"You don't need to say the 'L' word, Nic, I'm gonna fuck you anyway," I say playfully, quickly discarding my jeans. I hook my fingers over the waistband of my panties and slowly, teasingly pull them down and add them to the pile of clothes.

He looks me over, eyes lingering on my cunt. I always love this moment with a new acquaintance, the moment of realisation that they are actually going to feel the heat of my pussy. He circles me before stopping behind me and unhooking my bra. I feel his breath on the back of my neck and shiver in anticipation of what's to come.

Just touch me, please just touch me.

His hands latch on to my bra straps and draw them down my arms and on to the floor. I lean back into his broad chest as he brings his hands to my petite breasts, kneading my tender globes. Fingertips brush across my flesh before clasping my nipples and pinching them into hard ripe buds. He lets go and turns me around, now standing face to face. He undresses, stripping off his jeans and pants, adding to the mountain of clothes strewn across the bathroom and as my gaze rests on his exposed cock I smirk and say, "Yes, you can love me all you damn well like."

He lowers his head and his lips fuse with my own,

cushioning and comforting. The kiss is short, but sweet, as Nic heads towards the shower. Warm steam is already rising from the powerful showerhead, causing the bathroom to fill with a hazy glow. I follow him inside the cubicle and he pulls me close, slipping his arm around my waist and pulling me under the spray. Droplets of water dancing over his broad, tanned shoulders. I lean in to him, resting my forehead on his chest, and we stay like that for a long time. Minutes pass by and I finally look up to see him staring back at me with such want and desire. Succumbing to him at last, I grab his neck and slam his lips to mine.

The kiss is passionate, tongues exploring, teeth grazing, lips searching. He trails his fingertips along my spine, causing goose flesh to rise on my skin. I arch into his touch, his fingers dancing exotically across my back making my cunt ache for him.

"Fuck me, Nic," I pant.

"Fuck you? Are you serious?" He smirks and rests his hands on my hips. "I'm not going to fuck you, Mattie, you can get any of the guys to do that. No, I'm going to make love to you."

I don't understand why he wants me this way, but he does and the last thing I am going to do is shun him. I look down at the flesh of our lower bodies as his lips find my earlobe, "I want to fuck you Mattie, and there will be plenty of that I am sure, but for now I need to take this slowly. I need to savour every kiss of your lips, every touch of your silky skin, every groan that sounds from your throat. I need to worship you and show you what love is and how good sex can be when it's with someone who wants you."

My heart leaps for his, it aches to join with him and to fuse our bodies together, to become one. I recognise the look of pain, of a lonely soul finally finding a soul mate. He presses me up against the back of the shower and his cock presses shamelessly into my stomach. Sinking to my knees, I lick his length before taking him into my mouth, my hunger finally satisfied. He fists my hair, clutching handfuls of my sodden locks as he starts to slide his shaft down my throat. This is where I'm happy, on bended knee and ready to serve, providing the ultimate in pleasure.

"Enough, baby," He says and reluctantly withdraws his dick from between my lips.

Lifting me up, he grips my ass firmly and I wrap my legs around his waist, preparing for him to breach the lips of my cunt and fuck me at long last. I dig my nails into the taut flesh of his shoulders as I steady myself. Reaching between us with my free hand, I circle his length and guide him towards my entrance, slick with my own arousal. He presses his forehead to mine, moaning as his cock finds my wet flesh. I buck my hips towards him gently and feel him slide into me with ease, his hips grinding onto me as he fills me.

My pussy swallows him greedily, needing to be filled completely by this man. Throwing my head back against the glass of the shower, my eyes flutter closed with the pleasure of being worshipped so deliciously. Our breathing grows louder and faster as his thrusts quicken.

"I can't last much longer, Mattie," he says whilst slamming into me firmly, each thrust of his cock rubbing against that sweet spot inside my cunt.

I start to tremble, growing closer to climax as my inner muscles clench, milking Nic's cock as he slams into me again and again. As his teeth sink in to the flesh above my collarbone I lose control completely and feel myself begin to spill over the edge. My pussy tightens around him and I scream into the room, my orgasm bursting forth. A few long, smooth thrusts later and Nic spills into me, pumping hard before steadying himself by pressing against me, holding us both in place so we don't collapse to the floor of the shower.

Chapter Four

"What the hell has happened to you, Mattie?" Solène asks as we push our way into Voltage Dolls.

I thumb the samples that rest on the coffee table in the reception of this large tattoo parlour. "Eh?"

"Ever since you've been with Nic you've changed, we hardly ever see you and we miss you, ya know?"

I do know. They miss Mattie, the fun fuck. The easy fuck.

"You guys can get anyone you want to replace me, Sol, there are swarms of groupies that would kill to follow in my footsteps." My fingers stop on a black and white design, a large dragonfly. *There's something about that dragonfly,* I muse silently.

Brushing my bangs from my face, Solène looks at me sadly and grows serious. "We don't want anyone else, we want you."

"We?"

"All of us — me, Josh, Brandon, especially Bibi, we all miss you like fuckin' crazy." She bumps my shoulder playfully. "I know about you two by the way. She told me everything, before telling me how much she adores you. For fuck sake, Mattie, we all adore you!"

Shit. Love or sex; why did it always have to be such a compromise!?

Looking back down at the design, I make up my mind. It's time to be free.

"I want one," I announce proudly, taking the design to the front desk.

I need to escape the world for a while, surely Solène couldn't expect me to choose between Nic and my friends. I need to clear my mind, and what better way than with a new inking.

The sound of forty tattoo guns buzzing at once.

Fuck me.

My pussy weeps, hungry…thirsty…greedy for inkings past. My eyes are ablaze with desire as I survey every artist and every willing victim. I didn't plan to get a tattoo, but as soon as I see her I'm sold. The soft southern drawl and petite frame draw me in like a moth to a flame and as I rake my eyes over her scruffy dark hair and tanned skin, I'm letting her talk me into more needlework.

I thought she'd be gentle with such tiny hands and wide innocent eyes, but no. Nothing prepares me for the pain she's about to inflict upon my form. I flinch as the gun rocks into action, but as soon as that familiar scratch begins to drag across my skin I'm lost, transported into another world where it's just her and me, and guns and restraints. Lots and lots of restraints. And hair pulling. No kissing though. Biting, scratching, slapping, spitting…*spanking!* But no kissing.

Rough sex. Greedy sex. Hungry sex. It's just what I need at the moment; a simple fuck with no emotion and heartache.

She continues to stab at my ribs with the gun and all I can see as I look down at my four-inch biker heels is how good I would look in nothing but my delicate lace French knickers, those dirty boots, and a few seemingly random images dotted across my body. Dark black ink against creamy caramel flesh. I would look even better draped across her, my mouth to her cunt, my lips to hers, nipping at her clit before dipping my tongue between her folds and lapping at her like a smug feline.

She stops. I'm done. And as I look down at my newly tarnished flesh and the image that will burn into me forever I smirk, realising the one thing that matters above all else — the most important person in my life is me.

"I just need some time, Sol," I say as we exit the tattooist and prepare to go our separate ways.

She looks sad, "I hear ya, babygirl, but please…I miss you, I miss my best friend."

Guilt washes through me and I realise how selfish I've been of late, letting love snatch me away from all the people I care about. Heading back to my apartment, an overstuffed mailbox reminds me I haven't been there for a while. I begin to wonder whether it's love I need after all. Sure, Nic is amazing, but really, love or no love, can I ever just be with one person? I'm not sure I can.

The darkness of the quiet apartment dances over me. It washes away my day and lulls me into a state of bliss as it wraps me in its arms. Comforting me. Protecting me. The darkness is my light. In the darkness my smiles are their widest. In the darkness my eyes glimmer and shine, glittering into the black and beyond. In the darkness my fingers touch and tease, they twist and tweak, tapping at my pleasure spots. In the dark I dream. In the dark I am beautiful. In the dark I am free.

Sinking deep into the covers, I feel my mattress meld itself around the contours of my body. Suddenly, the bed dips and bounces as she falls on top of me. Fuck! Solène! She's let herself in. In a millisecond I know it's her. Her scent. Her touch. She doesn't even need to make a sound. I gaze at her through the darkness, my eyes twinkling, my smile wide and playful. Can she see me through the darkness? Can she see my desire for her bursting from my fingertips as they trail up and down her sides, tickling her copper skin? Can she see my chest rise and fall with the soft chuckles that spill from my mouth as I cup her breasts, revelling in the weight of them in my palms? Can she how much I want her still, that I haven't abandoned her?

I pull her to me, crashing her body to mine as my lips seek and find hers, devouring her. This is the kiss. *The* kiss. The one that is my undoing. I open my thighs wider and wrap my legs around her hips, pressing her into me. Our cunts meet, brushing against each other in the sweetest kiss. I weep. My pussy weeps. My clit swells and my pussy blossoms. Then it comes. The darkness. It washes over me. It leaves me sated and happy.

"Fuck, Mattie, I'm so glad to have you back," Solène

whispers against my lips as we come down from our high.

"You shouldn't have come, Sol," I say, unable to rid thoughts of Nic from my mind.

"I know you love him, Mattie, but this, now, with me, proves that you're meant to be free."

"Like you?"

She nods. "Exactly like me."

"But don't you crave love, Sol? Don't you hunger for the arms around you that keep you warm at night?"

She chuckles and it warms me slightly. "Oh, dear, dear Mattie, I have love. So, so much love. Love doesn't need to be exclusive to one person." She strokes my brow and I finally understand what she's saying."

"Ohhhh."

"Yeah, Oh."

"I think I need to talk to Nic."

Chapter Five

I walk in on Nic sitting on the sofa, reading intently from a sheet of paper. My first thought is that he's reading music or lyrics, maybe writing a new track, but then he holds out the paper in my direction. Something's not right about his expression, he seems serious and sombre, almost angry, though I'm not quite sure that's it. I can't read him yet. I don't know him well enough.

Taking the sheet from his hand I begin to read.

Sometimes in life you experience something that has a profound effect on the person you are. You experience something, and something inside you shifts. You realise that those fantasies that were always so strong, the ones that induced the most intense of orgasms, were actually nothing in comparison to the reality. Last year that happened to me.

I met someone.
I experienced something.
And something shifted.
I changed.

Now I will admit to myself, and perhaps to the eyes of a trusted few what my heart…my mind…and my body desire the most. My name is Matilda Harrison and these are my secrets untold....

I want to be desired *— I want to be something that somebody wants, to be lusted after. I want it to be my body that someone's fingers long to touch, my hair that somebody longs to run their fingers through, my lips that someone dreams of kissing, my eyes someone sees when they shut their own.*

I want to be fucked *— I want somebody to push me up against the wall, to smash their lips to mine, to fist my hair, to grip my throat tightly and squeeze gently until I grow lax and falter, to rip the clothes from my body, to scratch my flesh until welts rise, red and proud on my skin, to bite my skin until it breaks and I grow sore.*

I want to be nurtured *— I want to be cared for, to have someone who wants to protect me and keep me from harm, to be my friend, to respect me, to hold me close, caress my skin and kiss me sweetly as we share long nights of slow and tender love making. To smile at my successes and comfort me when I wobble.*

I want to be pushed *— I want someone who's fearless, who's unafraid to challenge me, to push my buttons, to see my fiery passion and tempestuous rage, to use me as I need to be used, to test my limits and appreciate my desire to submit. To take the strong-minded, stubborn woman and allow me to face my* *deepest, darkest desires and not feel disgust if I cry tears of shame and sadness. I want to be laid face down in a lavish hotel room and brought to my rawest form — to have my flesh cut deeply, slowly, lovingly to allow my blood to spill forth and let me feel the beautiful sting I still long for.*

I want to be your perfect slut *— I want to bow my head and kneel at your feet as you fasten the beautiful black collar around my neck. I want to part your puffy lips and feast upon your cunt as I gaze up at you through wide blue eyes, I want to lap at your chest like the perfect pussycat suckling at your teats, I want to be obedient, subservient, and punished for my indiscretions. I want to be spanked when I've failed you and spanked when I haven't. I want to be forced into climax, to be taught how to be a perfect woman for you. I want you to teach me how to give and how to receive as a perfect pet should. I am a pet who is born to serve and worship. Your pet, so adorable and willing.*

Shit.

"Where did you get this?"

"What does it matter? What the fuck is this, Mattie?"

I look to the floor, ashamed, though of what exactly I'm unsure. "What does it look like?"

"It looks like you need to come over here, kneel between my legs and tell me who the fuck you are and what the hell it is you want. No more secrets."

His words are harsh, but he's not angry. Confused perhaps, but not angry. He looks like a man who is full of questions, not someone who's about to kick me to the curb. I walk across the room and kneel between his legs as he insinuated for me to do so.

Lifting my chin with a finger, he asks, "Who was it written for?"

"Nobody."

He pinches my cheeks and repeats the question, "Who was it written for?"

"Them Nic, it was written for them. It was written for Solène and Bibi and Josh and Brandon and every other rock star I've ever fucked!"

He smiles. Why is he smiling? Shouldn't he be rife with jealousy?

"I've waited so long to find someone like you, Mattie, someone who is so fuckin' adorable, so lovable, yet so, so fuckable. Why would I deny the world of you?"

"Wh-a-at are you saying, that I'm free to fuck who I please?"

"That's exactly what I'm saying, and I will be with you every step of the way."

Thoughts of Nic and Solène flash into my mind, each pawing at me whilst others look on, willing participants in hedonistic debauchery. There I am, on all fours on the floor, the carpet rubbing painfully against my knees. I grip him, but how tightly I don't recall. Perhaps this is because my mind is a blur of arousal and desire, or perhaps because I am completely absorbed with the sucking of his cock.

Nic is more than I ever dreamt he could be, his hands gripping my hair tightly as he fucks my throat with long, slow strokes. I am gone, lost in a world where reality and fantasy begin to blur into one. The swollen head of his cock taps against the back of my throat, forcing me to gag and wretch. Mmmmmmmmmmmm…more. More, more, MORE!

"Every step?"

"There are things…people…I would like to experience too, with you, if you are okay with watching your man slide his dick into another woman of course?"

Throwing myself into his lap, I grin at him mischievously. "Are you kidding me? Hot!"

"As are you, baby," he smiles and kisses me quickly. "And I cannot wait to see this sweet little pussy of yours fucked raw."

And so continues my journey into life as a groupie, fucking my way from gig to gig, with Nic, the love of my life, with me for every step of the journey.

The Vicar's Organ

◆◆◆◆

by Percy Quirk

The Accompanist

Chapter One

My husband, unknown to him, would often accompany our lovemaking on the church organ. I would be face down on the bed, my skirt pushed up to my waist with my knickers and stockings bundled down against the backs of my knees, perspiration stinging my eyes as the Right Honourable Mr. Bertrand Creasey would first wet his cock in my flooded, yearning cunt and then work it deep into my ass. It became so that the music, these hymns that had endured hundreds of years as praise to my husband's God, were a part of the experience. It became so that, after some months of our meetings on a Sunday morning, even the sound of my husband practicing in the week — half-finished melodies, wrong notes, and occasional, playful tunes from the musicals thrown in — would fill me up with wanton sensations, my nipples suddenly sensitive against the cotton of my blouse, my stomach full of butterflies. I would get down on my knees, imagining my face level with the honourable Mr. Creasey's open flies, his fat, aggressive cock pushing through the open zip, his hand on the back of my head, and my eyes slowly closing as I lowered my mouth forward. Sometimes I could climax without touching myself, but I realise now that I have always been suggestible. I thought no such thing at the time.

I felt empowered by my sexuality, like a queen worshipped. But then, this was 1950 and all of us who had never left the mainland during the war were probably naïve.

My husband was the Vicar of St. Valentine's and, in all but name, was Mr. Creasey's employee. The church was maintained, as were the church buildings of several other neighbouring and nearby parishes, on the financial hand-outs provided by Mr. Creasey. As you can tell, the financial generosity displayed by Mr. Creasey was not, in our case, due solely to his charitable nature and it was probably six months into mine and my husband's relocation to St. Valentines that Mr. Creasey paid me a visit to explain the situation. Even then, I think, he had known my husband was absent by the sound of the church organ being played, the music rolling down the hill and over the village.

"Mrs. Evans," he said when I opened the door, momentarily removing his hat and then placing it back down on his head in a polite way that seems strange, almost silly now.

I invited him in and made him tea, chatting about inconsequential things while he moved around the sitting room, picking up our ornaments, turning them in his broad hands, and setting them back down again. I remember feeling uncomfortable then, seeing his expression of mild amusement as he fingered a picture from our wedding, my husband beaming and me dressed entirely in virginal white. I brought him his tea, after establishing that he took no sugar, and he took it from me. We stood there for a moment and then he slowly, deliberately, poured the tea all over the carpet and, when it was empty, casually smashed the cup in the fireplace.

I do not know if it was shock, or fear, but when it happened I was paralyzed, and could think of nothing to say.

"I'll keep it brief," Mr. Creasey said to me, calmly it seemed. "I own everything in this house. The water, the tea leaves, the cups, *you*.... Everything. And I can do what I like with things I own."

I was shaking. I wanted to call out but I was held silent. I realised for the first time that in spite of his florid complexion and rotund physique, Mr. Creasey was a large, powerful man. He was tall and broad, so that he did not have to work at that power, had been born with it. Even now, in his late forties and clearly emblematic of a lifetime of indulgence, he could have smashed me down in a second. And, I thought with a strange mixture of horror and excitement, he could have done the same to my slender, bookish husband.

"You ask the Vicar," he sneered. "You ask him what would happen without my patronage, Mrs. Evans. I won't take possession right now, you see, but you ask him that and see what he says. I have debts to collect elsewhere, so you'll see me in three days. You ask him before then and see how things are."

He did not say goodbye but let himself out, leaving me standing there in the middle of the sitting room, shaking, staring at the broken tea cup in the grate and the dark stain on the carpet nearby.

I cleaned up the mess, moving the rug over the stain, and made my husband's dinner. It was not long before he arrived home, musical scores tucked under his arm, and a smile of happy satisfaction on his face.

"Did you hear?" he asked me.

I had to confess that I had not. I did not continue on, to tell him that it was because I had been so preoccupied with Mr. Creasey's visit, but allowed him to speak instead.

"Not to worry," he said. "You will hear on Sunday. Some beautiful music, written by a local man. An ex-soldier, I think. Really quite splendid."

He gave an involuntary laugh, as he often did when he felt pleased with the world.

"I think he was a Sergeant," William continued. "Royal Engineers. He's offered to give me a hand restoring the organ."

"That will be nice, dear," I said.

I led him into the kitchen and served his dinner. We chatted about the fete, which was due that summer, and how I might get involved in the organisation.

"You'll have to help Lady Creasey," he told me. "She's in charge. It's the only thing that really brings her out into the community, you know, and it's important we make the right impression with her."

"Are the Creaseys so important for us?" I asked him. "Do we need to dance to their tune? What if I wanted to do my own organising?"

He dropped his knife and folk. There was a sharp clatter as they fell against the plate, and he fixed me with his eyes, a look of genuine concern passing over his face.

"They are *very* important," he said to me, and I felt peculiarly conflicting emotions. "This church, and my position here, could not exist without their charity. We must not do anything to anger them — nothing at all."

I started to speak but he held up his hand.

"You'll do what Mrs. Creasey tells you to do on the fete," he said. "We'll do nothing to anger them, Alice, nothing at all."

And so that, as my husband might have said, was that.

Chapter Three

Three days later, on the Friday evening, my husband was scurrying around the Vicarage, looking for his umbrella and his car keys.

"For God's sake!" he exclaimed. "Why does Creasey have to come up with this idea now? A bloody Vicar's dinner over in Uphamstead?! I couldn't think of anything more boring if I tried.

"And," he added, "It's not as if Creasey's bothering to go himself."

He shook his head with a slight, resigned smile, and kissed me on the cheek.

"You look nice," he said. "Anyway, I should be back about twelve I guess. Don't wait up."

And he was gone.

Mr. Creasey's knock did not come until an hour later by which time I was frantic with apprehension, perched on the edge of a chair in the sitting room, wondering what exactly our local parliamentarian had in mind. I hesitated before opening the front door, but then realised there was little point in avoiding the act, now that the decision had been made. I had my husband's blessing, if indirectly, and as far as blessings go a Vicar's should carry some weight.

He was standing in the doorway, a large black silhouette with the dim lights of the houses and the round white eye of the moon behind him. Not being able to see his face, the shadow that he made across the hallway, the essential *darkness* of him, caused me to shudder in a way that was both fearful and excited.

"Little pig, little pig," he said. "Won't you let me in." It was not a question. I could hear amusement and scorn in his tone.

"Certainly, sir," I said, stepping back and holding the door for him. His big feet, smart brown shoes slightly dirty from the wet road, stepped over the threshold and marked the carpet. I could not look at his face, so high above it seemed, but looked downward instead, either from shame or by some kind of natural deference. I saw the muddy marks he left on the floor, and was aware of his bulk as he passed me; an enormous bear of a man. I felt so small, so vulnerable, as I closed the door and followed him obediently into my own living room or, as I suddenly realised, *his* living room that my husband and I occupied only as tenants.

"I like it when you call me 'Sir'," he said. "From now on you can call me 'Sir' or 'Mr. Creasey'."

His back was to me, but his shoulders started to move up and down and I realised he was chuckling.

"Actually I have a better idea," he said. "You can address me as 'Mr. Creasey, sir', at all times. Do you understand?"

"Yes, Mr. Creasey, sir." I said.

He turned around slowly and looked down at me, took my chin in one of his large hands, and lifted my face.

"I am not going to treat you well, Mrs. Evans," he said slowly, calmly, his eyes looking into mine. For some reason I could not look away. "I expect complete obedience. If I receive obedience then you can expect to be treated like one of my horses; groomed, fed, housed, and ridden. If you buck me, if you act up, then you can expect to be thrashed and tamed, like one of my horses. And I love my horses, Mrs. Evans, they are such beautiful creatures — it is only that beauty is nothing to me unless it is in my possession. Do you understand?"

"Yes Mr. Creasey, sir."

"There's a good filly," he smiled. "Now you can fetch me a brandy and undress, in that order."

"Yes Mr. Creasey, sir."

He sat down in my husband's chair as I poured him the brandy with trembling fingers, still careful not to spill any. Something in me was certain that errors like this, like a spilt drink, would not go unnoticed or unpunished. I brought the drink over and he took it from me without a word so that I was standing in front of him, empty handed, in a state on mild shock realising that the next thing I had to do was present myself to him naked. He said nothing, but from the look that was starting to fix on his face I could tell that he was becoming angry and impatient. Almost without thinking, I started to undress.

I started with my shoes, kneeling down and

unbuckling each one, placing them side by side next to the sofa. My blouse was next, and his purposeful gaze impelled me not to hesitate with any of the buttons, and when the buttons were unfastened I did not hesitate before removing it completely. I was going to lay it over the back of the sofa when I heard Mr. Creasey say, "Fold it properly. I paid for that blouse." So I folded it carefully, flushing full in the face, ashamed like a school girl that I had been caught treating my things carelessly, and angry that I had been reminded again of our dependence on him. I unfastened my bra and folded it in two, placing it on top of the folded blouse that Mr. Creasey had paid for, that was on the sofa that we had bought with money from Mr. Creasey, and which sat in a house that Mr. Creasey owned. I turned and dropped my arms, presenting my breasts to him so he could see that I understood; that he owned me too.

"You're a horny little slut, Mrs. Evans," he said to me, smirking. My nipples were dark and erect. I could already imagine his hands on my breasts, roughly kneading them, hurting and exciting me. "Get on with it," he said, gesturing impatiently with his hand.

I unfastened my skirt, again folded it, and laid it next to the blouse on the sofa. I was down to my stockings and knickers.

"Leave them," he told me. "I will only use your mouth today."

He set down the drink and stood up. From his pocket he drew out a length of dark ribbon.

"Turn around," he said. I turned until my back was to him and then felt him take my arms, pulling them together, and the soft ribbon being wound about my wrists until my hands were bound together. He was clever — the ribbon was soft and would not leave a mark. There would be nothing to suggest to my husband that anything had happened. I felt appalled but also something else, maybe admiration — maybe even gratitude.

"Kneel," he said to me, and I knelt.

"Turn," he said and, on my knees, I turned.

He was sitting back down in my husband's chair but his flies had been opened and his erect penis, thick and long, was standing out from his trousers. It seems unfair to compare it directly with that of my husband, only to say that it was in keeping with the general scale of the man; that it was in keeping with his large, powerful physique.

"Mrs. Evans," he said to me quietly. "The best whores can bring a man to orgasm in seconds using only their mouth. Right now you are probably not the best of whores, a cheap whore if you will, though I expect you to be eager to learn."

He leaned forward and touched my cunt through the silk of my knickers.

"Dripping wet," he said to me. "That must be a little embarrassing for you, Mrs. Evans, but you're not judged here. Your feelings and thoughts, things like pride, are inconsequential to me. I am interested only in your actions, in your performance."

Again, that strange sense of gratitude. Although his indifference to me was demeaning, it seemed preferable to a more personal, a more specific need to humiliate me, which could have been more dangerous. This way, as long as he had no emotional attachment to me, things could remain contained. As long as I did as he asked, my marriage and my position would not be threatened — at least this was my hope, and that hope fluttered gratefully in my breast as he described his lack of interest in me as anything other than a proficient whore.

"So," he continued, sitting back. "Work yourself over here Mrs. Evans and show me what a good little cock sucker our Vicar's wife really is."

"Yes Mr. Creasey, sir," I replied and moved forward, my mouth opening wide, perhaps a string of wanton saliva running down my chin, focussed on nothing else in the world beyond pleasing my husband's benefactor, the Right Honourable Mr. Bertrand Creasey, who at that moment was laughing uncontrollably.

The Diva

Chapter Four

The less I say about the more intimate details between myself and Mr. Creasey the better, however I will confirm that my "training" continued and, following my husband's unknowing approval, I felt no particular compulsion to resist. That is to say that any attempt I made to resist was quickly quashed in such a way as I eventually came to feel childish in having raised an objection in the first place. Mr. Creasey was very clear on the consequences of disobedience and on several occasions I reached a point where I was convinced that he would reveal my sins to my husband while at the same time ripping away our livelihood, stripping William of his ability to serve God. At such moments the horrible trap I was in became acutely perceived, so that I bucked like a chicken in the arms of a farmer, helpless to stop it's neck from being wrung. I could almost see the iron bars holding me in. Having been led like a fool into my cage my choice was now to continue betraying my husband, or to bring about his destruction.

You can imagine from the brief glimpse of Mr. Creasey's appetites that I have so far allowed you that the acts I was subjected to, and ordered to perform, were acutely humiliating, deeply sexual, and imbued at the same time with an impersonality that stripped me of the dignity even of being a victim. He drew my lust out while at the same time acknowledging me as nothing more than an object, at best a pet; a panting dog waiting for the click of his fingers.

At the same time I followed publically the path of a dutiful Vicar's wife: visiting my neighbours when they were unwell; offering a childcare service on Sundays for those that wished to attend mass without distraction; tending my husband and his, our, Mr. Creasey's house. These duties led me, a few short weeks after the reality of my position at the Vicarage became clear, to the preparation of the fete where I was to encounter the wives of the Vicars from the neighbouring parishes, along with Lady Creasey.

"She's a wonderful woman," Mrs. Heffer giggled nervously. As well as being the wife of the Reverend from St. Bartholomew's, she was one of the longest serving volunteers on the fete committee, having been in the area for ten years. She took me under her wing, introducing me to the other volunteers, and was now leading me across the hallway of Creasey House to the drawing room, which doubled as the headquarters of the planning committee for the upcoming fete. She opened the door and stood back against it, although it became immediately apparent that my squeezing past her would be embarrassing for us both; she was, let us say, on the larger side. She flushed a beetroot red and carried on through the door so that I could enter.

"Lady Creasey," she announced. "This is Mrs. Evans"

I found myself confronted by a small semi-circle of seated women, all focussed on a single, high-backed chair, rather like a throne, in which sat the most coldly beautiful woman that I had, and have, ever encountered. Her dark hair hung sheer like a black curtain down her long, straight back. Her cheeks were touched with rouge, but otherwise her face was pale and fine, although not delicate — it was fine like the sharp edge of a razor. She offered me an amused smile and I was immediately struck by a sense that she could see into my thoughts, knew everything, could see me on my back, my tongue out, slicking her husband's anus, as if she had been there herself. And, rather than appalled or sickened, she was merely amused.

"Do sit down, Mrs. Evans" she said, offering me her hand. "We've saved you a seat."

Not knowing the proper way to behave I took her hand and risked a small curtsey. This gave her cause to laugh, and the other women present immediately joined in.

"There won't be any need for anything like that, Mrs. Evans," she said. "You are already doing me an incredible service just by being here. You all are," she added, looking around the room. All of the women there smiled coyly, fingers over their mouths, and looked down at the burgundy carpet.

The rest of the afternoon passed uneventfully enough, with Mrs. Heffer providing the tea. She did not seem to want the servants to wait on her, as if it made her uncomfortable. So, with Lady Creasey's permission, she shooed them away and catered for us herself. It obviously gave her pleasure, somehow, to be servile, particularly to Lady Creasey.

As for the Lady herself, I was entranced and puzzled. Although I was, and still am, an attractive woman, it did not seem credible that a man with such a wife should take pleasure from the company of someone like me. I found myself strangely flattered by Mr. Creasey's attentions, that he should have selected me for such attention when he had this exquisite creature with whom to share his marriage bed. And at the same time I felt no competition with her, in fact I felt defeated from the start. She was the sort of woman that men die and kill for; she had that kind of beauty, that kind of poise, that kind of aloof sensuality and mischievous intelligence.

"Didn't I tell you she was wonderful," Mrs. Heffer said to me as we were leaving. "We're very lucky to have such a Lady as part of our group. She gives the kind of steady leadership we need and we simply couldn't do without her."

I nodded silently, not really clear as to why seven grown women needed leadership, but then Mrs. Heffer was not a leader herself. She was the type that was grateful when someone told her what to do, as it took the burden of responsibility away from her. She was a one of those unimaginative, kindly women that one immediately likes and immediately despairs of. I bid her good night and went home to my husband, who was brooding in the sitting room.

"Good evening, dear," I said, kissing his forehead. "Did you have a productive day?"

"Very," he remarked, somewhat drily. "Sergeant

Haylock has started his work on the church organ."

"That's good, isn't it?" I asked, removing my coat.

"I'm not sure," William replied thoughtfully. "I didn't really see the need, but then he explained some things... Things are less clear."

He winced and looked down into the fireplace, as if disturbed by some inner torment.

"He writes beautiful music," William said, eventually. "To play it properly, we need to make some updates to the organ. I'm not sure talent like that can come from God...."

This final cryptic remark I left alone. It was late and I was tired, and I could see that William was also exhausted. Whatever he had been discussing with the Sergeant had taken his toll. I thought it foolish to care so much about a silly piece of music, but it did cross my mind that if the organ were out of commission for any length of time, Mr. Creasey would be able to visit me less. I surprised myself by immediately thinking of ways that I could engineer further meetings, but then stopped myself. I would not become his accomplice.

I had to dress in the bathroom with the door locked so as to hide the marks that Mr. Creasey had left across my breasts and buttocks earlier that week, but William was asleep by the time I had finished brushing my teeth and slid into bed beside him.

Chapter Five

The day of the actual fete was cloudless and hot. Myself and the rest of the committee were expected to be at the green for seven a.m. and indeed, Lady Creasey was there herself; counting us all in and greeting us with a cordial hello and a clipboard, on which we all found fastened a personalized checklist of our duties for the day. All of the Vicar's wives read them with earnest attention until Mrs. Heffer gave out a small gasp. When everyone looked at her she flushed red with embarrassment, as she so often did, and gave everyone a polite smile.

"Looks like I'm going to be very busy today," she said. The other wives nodded and continued to look at their own checklists, but for my part there was something strange about the whole exchange. What could have been on Mrs. Heffer's checklist that had caused such a response? And why did I get the impression that I was the only wife there who did not seem to express in their faces a kind of relieved understanding? Well, perhaps not Mrs. Christie from St. Rudolphs, who seemed a trifle consternated, but then Mrs. Christie was a stick-thin, grey-haired woman, and always seemed consternated about something.

Still, we set about it. My main duties were to man

the cake stall with Lady Creasey, something that was both an honour a challenge. As it was my first fete, Lady Creasey wanted to get to know me better, possibly to assess me, but it was also vital (as Mrs. Heffer had explained to me at great length) to assess my abilities in the baking department. The provision of cake to her husband's parish was a critical task for a Vicar's wife, and it was understood amongst the women that, as they say about men, the quickest way to the parishioners' hearts is through their stomachs. Clearly it was the quickest way to Mrs. Heffer's heart, from her extra pounds, but I could see how this would be also true for the common men and women of the parish. I had so many reasons to be ashamed by now that anything which might help my husband received my utmost zeal, as if a tray of perfectly iced fairy cakes could be set against my infidelity, my lies, and my willing degradation.

We set out the table, Lady Creasey and myself, and covered the cakes with greaseproof paper or cake lids that Lady Creasey had brought from the kitchen up at Creasey House. As we had some time before the fete opened to the rest of the diocese, we took some time for tea and conversation. I was terribly nervous.

"You've done such a wonderful job, Lady Creasey," I said.

"Oh, Mrs. Evans," she replied. "You have no idea how grateful to you I am. To all of the wives, but to you especially this year. These things are not that savoury, you understand…."

"Well, they aren't supposed to be are they, Lady Creasey?" I asked, confused. "They are supposed to be sweet."

"I suppose you're right…" she said, and then laughed. "Oh, you mean the cakes? Of course, of course. Very sweet."

For the second time that day, and for the countless time since I had moved to the Vicarage, I felt that there was something that I was missing; some secret fact that I was not privy to. It was strange that I should feel this way, as to the best of my knowledge it was myself who was lying, and myself who was withholding things from Lady Creasey. Perhaps it was my insecurity, or something to do with our difference in class, but I always had the feeling that Lady Creasey knew everything that had happened between her husband and myself, all of my thoughts and feelings, my shame, but also knew so much else besides; that there was another narrative beyond my simple infidelity, and the rather complex sexual cruelty of her husband.

As if on cue at that moment Mr. Creasey himself arrived, escorting a group of young men who were carrying a wide, low-rimmed barrel along the central aisle of stalls toward a big marquee tent at the end.

"Come on, lads," he was shouting. "Put your backs into it."

As he passed us he turned and saw Lady Creasey, and then his eyes fell on me. It was extraordinary. At first, on seeing his wife, a look of incredible discomfort crossed over his features, as if he were being subjected to some intense emotional pain but then, on seeing me, his expression transformed immediately into the familiar one of naked, brutal lust. The oddity, the shocking thing, was that it must have been as plain as day to his wife. I quickly glanced at her but she was still smiling calmly at her husband. It seemed that she gave him a sharp, discrete nod, and he came over to us.

"Come along, Mrs. Evans," he said to me. "There's something I want your help with over in that there tent."

I looked immediately at Lady Creasey.

"Run along, Mrs. Evans," she said. "I'll be alright here for a few minutes."

Mr. Creasey took my hand and led me through the stalls to that large tent, where the men were just laying the barrel down on the grass. Also in the tent was a contraption involving a stool and a large white circle with a red dot in the middle.

"Give us some privacy," Mr. Creasey barked at the men, and they left us alone. The canvas of the tent was quite thick so we were afforded the privacy that Mr. Creasey had asked for and which, like some dog trained to salivate at the sound of a bell, I also immediately craved.

"And how are you this morning, Mrs. Evans?" he asked.

I curtseyed, as I had been trained to do, bowing my head just a little and replying, "Very well thank you, Mr. Creasey, sir."

"Very good," Mr. Creasey grinned. "I have some

instructions for you, Mrs. Evans."

My mind, as was usual, sparked with different fantasies. There were so many things I wanted him to insist on, so many things I feared he might do, and so many times already that I had been surprised by the imagination of his wishes.

"Yes, Mr. Creasey, sir," I responded, curtseying again.

"I want you to hoist up your skirts and piss in that barrel," he said. "I don't want you taking a break from the cake stall now. I might want some cake later, and I don't like queues. More to the point, I won't have Lady Creasey taxed."

I must have hesitated, as I remember being momentarily puzzled, and because the long cane he carried around like a baton stung my buttocks with a hard crack.

"Yes, Mr. Creasey, sir," I said with a trembling voice, eyes watering from my stinging cheeks, and did as I was told.

It felt so base, relieving myself while he stood over, watching. It was also difficult to keep the stream away from the hem of my skirt, my petticoat, my shoes and stockings. I let myself go in small, controlled bursts, and there was something about doing this that made the moment more intimate, and Mr. Creasey's violation of that moment all the more shaming. I had no handkerchief to wipe myself, and he offered me none, so I merely dropped my skirts, stepped out of the barrel, and curtseyed.

"Good slut," Mr. Creasey said. "Now point my cock into the barrel."

I smiled broadly ("Yes, Mr. Creasey, sir") and

unfastened his trousers. At least, I thought to myself, I will get to touch him. I lovingly extricated his long, broad cock from his underpants and pointed it over the rim of the barrel. I kept my face near to it and my mouth slightly open, as I knew he liked that. I hoped too that such proximity might incite him to force something sexual on me, while at the same maintaining enough distance so as not to run the risk of catching some of his piss as he relieved himself into the barrel. His stream made a dull, heavy sound against the wood and it took him a long time to complete. Eventually it was over and I shook him off before, disappointedly, placing his penis back inside his pants.

I found it hard to believe this was all I had been called for. Did he not want my body? My cunt, my ass, my mouth…. Even just to be brought to climax with my hands or breasts? I was so disappointed and it must have shown on my face.

"Don't worry, Mrs. Evans," he said. "I'll give you a good fucking very soon, just not now."

"Yes, Mr. Creasey, sir," I said, bending my knees slightly. It reminded me of our first night at the Vicarage, when he had used only my mouth. He was always withholding, knowing how much my body wanted to feel him, to be overpowered, to be reduced to something bestial. I was excited then, tingling in my stomach, worried not to look into his face in case he mocked my desire, a desire so strong it was becoming almost indistinguishable from…. No, it could not be. We were both married. He felt nothing, nothing for me, so I could not feel real emotion for him. I had to maintain this — whatever *this* was — on a physical level only.

But as I looked at him my heart was beating hard, and my cunt was so aroused I was sure that anyone standing close would be able to smell that I was in heat. *I want you*, my eyes were saying, *take me and use me and destroy me, only let me make you happy*. Mr. Creasey saw my look and stopped laughing. A curious, soft smile fluttered on his lips.

"Come to the old barn a three o'clock sharp," he said to me, gesturing with his head. "Now run along and do whatever my wife tells you."

I stood there, my eyes glazed, staring upward into his sneering, ruddy face.

"Do you understand?!" he repeated angrily, and I came back to myself.

"Of course, Mr. Creasey, sir" I said, curtseyed, and left the tent. Whatever surprise had been promised for later there was a new surprise for me as I arrived at the cake stall: I realised that I hated Lady Creasey.

You have probably seen what I did not at that time: that I was infatuated with Mr. Creasey and possibly, probably, falling in love with him. You might think that I had sunk very low, but we are not nearly at the end of my story and I regret to tell you that I sank again, more than once, before the end. At lunchtime, though, my husband came to collect me for a walk around the fete and Lady Creasey allowed me half an hour to do so. Mr. Creasey was there as well, loitering with his lips fixed in a smirk; a look that, at that point, I found strangely attractive. My husband and I passed him as we moved away from the cake stall.

"Good day, Mr. Creasey, sir," I said, giving a very gentle bend of my knee. In truth I was becoming very frustrated, both sexually and emotionally, by his offhand treatment. I had spent the morning with his wife obeying every one of her silly little instructions, playing the good wife, smiling at the customers for the stall and making small talk, but all the time hating her and wanting him.

"You do look flushed," William said to me as we stood by the hoopla stall. "Are you feeling quite alright?"

I cannot remember what I truly felt at that moment, whether it was annoyance at his scrutiny or something else.

I would like to say that his concern melted me, that I was freed from Mr. Creasey's psychological grip, and confessed everything to my husband. I did not. I may have wanted to but all I can remember from that early part of the day was a sense of heightened sexuality, almost obsession.

At any rate, before I could answer, we were joined by my husband's friend, the soldier. He was a tall, handsome man with a patch over one eye, presumably hiding some injury from the war.

"Good day, madam," he said respectfully, and kissed my hand. So like a dog in heat was I that even such a cordial gesture made me want him, or anyone, to take me, there and then, in the dirt.

"Good day, Mr...?" I left the name hanging. I could not remember my husband having told me.

"Haylock," he said. "Sergeant Adam Haylock."

"Creasey House used to be called Haylock Hall," I said, remembering something that Mrs. Heffer had told me some weeks before.

"Indeed it did," he said, and smiled. I was intrigued by the patch over his eye, and what might lie beneath. When he smiled the creases around that eye, visible in part, created strange and unusual patterns.

"My husband says that you are doing a wonderful job with the organ," I remarked, thinking that it was expected of me. "And also that you are a wonderful composer."

"I dabble," he admitted, modestly.

"Will we hear some of your music, Mr. Haylock!?" I

exclaimed. "I would love to hear it. If you are as good as my husband tells me you are, it must be wonderful."

William and Mr. Haylock looked at each other cryptically and smiled between themselves.

"I'm sure you'll hear some of Sergeant Haylock's music very soon," William said to me, taking my arm. "It may not be to your taste, perhaps, but we will see."

"Oh, don't be so rude, William," I scolded him, but to my surprise they both laughed.

"Let's have a go at this game," William said, after we bid farewell to the Sergeant. He pointed to a stall where you had to throw rubber balls into the mouth of a painted clown, for which you could win a lamb joint, a bouquet of lavender, or a teddy bear.

Mr. Heffer was managing the stall and, on seeing me with my husband, called loudly to me.

"Mrs. Evans!" he called. "You should definitely have a go! Show us how it's done!"

Then he turned to the small crowd and ushered for them to let me through.

"Three balls for you," he said, handing me a small seaside bucket with the balls inside.

"Thank you, Reverend Heffer," I said.

"Reverend Jones," he corrected me, looking sheepish and reddening like his wife. "My name is Jones."

I was puzzled. He was certainly Mrs. Heffer's husband, as I had seen them together on several occasions, so it seemed odd that they should not have the same surname.

I did not know what to make of it, but at that moment I had more important things to worry about. I looked back over my shoulder at William, who gave me a little nod to continue.

I won a bouquet of lavender, which William took from me as I was heading back to work on the cake stall. I had some misgivings as I walked back, puzzled by the looks exchanged between William and Sergenat Haylock. I was half sure that a similar look had passed between William and Reverend Heffer, or Jones, or whatever his name was. In spite of these things, however, my mind was primarily occupied by Mr. Creasey and the rough, exquisite violation that I could expect later that day when I met him at the barn.

Lady Creasey looked up as I arrived, and smiled.

"Good to see you, Mrs. Evans," she said. "At last I can drop some of my load onto your willing shoulders."

Of course you can, I thought, having one particular load in mind.

Chapter Seven

We are drawing close to the moment when the full extent of what had been happening at Creasey House became known to me, but first there was the penultimate indignity that I was forced to endure. I had been a betrayer and I was betrayed. Looking back it seems only natural and right that this is what would happen, and in many ways is what *should* have happened. In my defence, should you feel the need to judge, I would only say that life is a complex thing and that love, or lust, is life at its most intense.

I went to the back of the barn as Mr. Creasey had instructed, every nerve ending in my body anticipating his firm, cruel touch. I arrived at three o'clock as I had been told to do and waited as patiently as I was able, worrying my rosary in a way that I am sure many of you will think is blasphemous. I was not praying with them and, if I was, my prayers were for something entirely at odds with their purpose. There was nothing spiritual in me at that moment; I was all animal.

I waited a further five, then ten, minutes. I could not bring myself to leave and nor could I bring myself to rebuke Mr. Creasey, even in my thoughts. I felt that he would see inside my mind and it would displease him. I waited five more minutes and, just I was about to slouch dejectedly off to my husband, like the rough beast I was, I heard the sound of talking from inside the barn. I would have paid no mind to it but the timbre of the male voice, deep and gravelly, could only have been Mr. Creasey, and he was talking with a woman.

I pressed my eye to a gap in the wooden walls of the barn and saw straight away that it was Mrs. Heffer.

"I must say, Mrs. Heffer, that you have excelled yourself over the last few years," Mr. Creasey was saying.

Mrs. Heffer, to my dismay, curtseyed and said:

"Thank you, my lord and master."

"Do you remember when you came here at first?" he continued. "A skinny whip of a lass from Brighton, ready to turn away from her less than savoury past and embrace a new life with a man of the cloth. Such fine intentions, wouldn't you say, Mrs. Heffer?"

"Yes, my lord and master."

"But we saved you from that, didn't we Mrs. Heffer? We fed you up and gave you a new name and now look at you, my own little bovine beauty. Are you grateful, Mrs. Heffer?"

"Yes, my lord and master."

"I know you are, Mrs. Heffer, and so is Mr. Jones no doubt. And that is why I have chosen this special day to give you a reward. What do you say to that, Mrs. Heffer?"

"Thank you, my lord and master."

She dropped heavily to her knees in front of him and pressed her lips gently against the patent leather of his right shoe, and then repeated the same gesture with his left shoe. Inside her summer dress her corpulent body heaved with sexual energy. You could see the outward dents of her large nipples pressing against the cotton, and she bobbed restlessly in her kneeling position. I was horrified but found myself unable to speak or to leave, in fact powerless to do anything except watch what would unfold.

"You may stand and lift up your dress," Mr. Creasey said to her. She did so and I could see that she wore no under garments as well as no brassiere. She wore only stockings beneath her dress. She held the hem patiently above her waist, her mouth slightly open, panting, a sheen of sweat glistening upon her bright red cheeks. Her thick thighs bulged at the tops of her stockings like a cake with too much icing.

"Turn around and bend over," Mr. Creasey said, and of course she did so. Her enormous breasts now hung down in front of her and I could see from my position that her pubic hair had been completely shaven. Mr. Creasey stepped into view, his flies open and his enormous cock straining forward towards the bending woman's wet, swollen lips. He pushed himself inside of her in one rough thrust and Mrs. Heffer, with a groan of primal pleasure, was sent forward onto her knees again, her dress up her back and her rump offered up like two wide, white moons of flesh. Mr. Creasey came down with her, thrusting and growling, grabbing her hair with one hand and the other circling around her body to play with her swinging breasts.

I could endure it no longer. Stronger than the arousal

that I could not help but feel as I watched them copulate so roughly, both of them taking such immense pleasure in the act, was the sense of abandonment, of betrayal, of my own stupidity. My brain would not let me comprehend it. As I started to turn away, eyes blindly searching in front of me for some salvation, for some way of believing that Mr. Creasey felt about me as I did about him, I heard Mr. Creasey demanding in his sex-choked voice:

"Say thank you in your real voice, Daisy, there's a good girl!"

I broke into a run, tripping and falling but always moving forwards, away from the sounds of Mr. Creasey's laughter, the slap of his loins against Mrs. Heffer's creamy, corpulent ass.

"Moooo," Mrs. Heffer sang, breaking into a giggle. "Mooooohooohooo."

I turned the corner of the barn and there was a skull staring at me — no it was Mrs. Christie, laughing unkindly — and then I fell forward toward the ground. The fall was long and slow, the blades of grass rising beside and above me like slender green towers, darkness only at their base, and into which I gladly swam.

When I woke, the very first thing that I was aware of was a broken heart, the second was Lady Creasey's face smiling down at me, and the last was the unusual setting in which I found myself. We were in the gallery of the church, above the congregation pews, directly facing the broad pipes of the church organ which were, thankfully, quiet. The noise in the upper gallery was unbearable when the organ was in full tilt, the musical notes of such extreme volume that they became almost indistinguishable and seemingly ran together. At such volumes it was impossible to hear the music, one had only the opportunity to feel it.

"How are you feeling, Mrs. Evans?" Lady Creasey asked me. "Mrs. Christie brought you to me. It seems like it may be time for some explanations, before things start getting exciting."

I was lying on a wooden bench, broader than the pews below, with my head resting on a pillow. I was exhausted and confused. I kept picturing different acts that I had performed, or had been performed on me, over the last months. Interspersed with these, as if there was a film projecting into my head, was the sight of Mr. Creasey entering Mrs. Heffer — or I suppose I should say Mrs. Jones — at the barn, her shameless delight which so closely resembled my own, and the disturbing subtext of sustained cruelty that lay in the words exchanged between the two of them. I felt like something had shattered inside me, that some part of me, at full stretch for a sustained period, had now snapped. Perhaps this was not a broken heart, and only the aftermath of disillusionment; a breakdown of sorts, surely.

Lady Creasey fed me sugary tea. We weren't alone in the gallery. In the background, busy with something out of sight, was the soldier I had seen with William at the Vicarage, then at the fete; the Soldier who wrote the music. Adam Haylock. He did not seem interested in us, however, and continued about his work.

"I owe you an explanation," Lady Creasey said eventually, her wide green eyes projecting some kind of strange radiance; the afterglow of some great emotion perhaps, or the look of a child who unboxes her present on Christmas day to find that it is a full of faeries. It was with this look of sublime exultation on her face that she told me the full story of what was happening at Creasey House.

"Bertrand was not my first husband," she began. "I knew him from childhood but it was his best friend, Adam Haylock, that I fell in love with and married. To tell the truth, I had never much cared for Bertrand Creasey whose manner, as I am sure you are by now aware, was not always befitting a man of his social standing. However, this was not particularly relevant then, as I was married and Bertrand was very much Adam's friend, or a least I thought. Then came the war and the two of them went away to fight. Adam, being two years into his training as a Vicar, became a battalion Chaplain for the Royal Engineers.

"Adam did not return and it was Bertrand who arrived at my door one cool November day to inform me that Adam had died during intense fighting south of Arnheim. I did not know where Arnheim was, whether the battle had been won, or what type of death Adam had endured, only that he was gone and that I would have to live the rest of my life without him. I was destroyed and collapsed. Bertrand carried me through to the drawing room, much as you were carried here, and lay me down on the sofa to recover. It was while I was lying there that he told me Adam's dying wish.

"He said that Adam had asked him to take care of me, to make sure that I was safe. He told me that Adam, in his last words, had told Bertrand that he was the only man whom he could bear to be with me. He had urged Bertrand to return and fill his place."

Lady Creasey paused to present me with an awful sneer. For the first time since we had met her composure was breached and I saw in her face a look of extreme bitterness and hatred. She collected herself quickly, seeing my shock, and patted my hand.

"At first he did not push the matter and merely cared for me," she continued. "I forgot about my dislike for him and was filled with gratitude. This, combined with my love for my husband and what I was assured was his dying wish, I consented to marry Bertrand Creasey when he proposed to me in the Autumn of the following year. I did not want another man except Adam, and the war seemed to have changed Bertrand into a gentleman whom I could at least care for, and be a wife to, even if I did not love him. The very first night of our marriage changed all of that irreversibly.

"I was taken in my wedding gown to the master bedroom and, where I had expected tenderness and perhaps the gentle love-making of two familiar friends, I was greeted by something very different. I was tied to the bed, face down in the pillows, and…. Creasey…."

She turned her head away from me, looking towards the soldier, still fixing something near to the organ pipes. He seemed not to have heard and instead started whistling to himself, some jolly army tune. At the same time I could hear the main door to the church open and close, and the voices of two or more men. It was impossible to distinguish who they were or what they were saying because of the quiet tones and the echo of the church. I started to sit up but Lady Creasey kept her hand on my shoulder and eased me gently back down.

"I'm nearly finished, dear," she assured me, so I stayed where I was and listened.

"After that night Mr. Creasey found my door always locked and a revolver always in my handbag. We continued to live in the same house, and I had no wish to inform the local people of my situation. The shame for me personally, as well as the legacy of my dead husband's name, would not allow it. I lived in married celibacy and a kind of unhappy dread. It became apparent to me that Creasey, in spite of his horrific failings, was in love with me. It was just that his sexuality, his mind, were perverse and corrupt. He equated sex with cruelty so I, seeing the possibilities inherent within his mental flaw, endeavoured to treat him as cruelly as I knew how. I had protected my money and restricted him to an allowance. I humiliated him in front of the servants, and kept him out of my bedroom. Gradually his love, as I suspected it might, turned to a kind of worship.

"However, his appetites did not go unsatisfied. Unknown to me at the time he began to exert an oppressive influence over a Vicar's wife from one of the parishes we support. By the time I learned of his actions it was quite advanced and the woman, when I confronted her, bizarrely did not wish the relationship to end. I tried to understand the woman but eventually felt only contempt for her. You have met Mrs. Christie, no doubt? Well, it was that stupid woman who began everything.

"But still, as a pragmatist I realised that, as long as Creasey could find an outlet for his deviant lusts, I would be much safer in the manor house. If I denied him, it would only be a matter of time before his desires would be uncontrollable. In short, we came to an arrangement regarding the wives of the local Vicars."

I hated her again. I hated the suggestion that Mr. Creasey was really in love with her, and that he was only with me by her consent. Even worse, she seemed to be suggesting that I was nothing more than a way to keep his basest instincts in check, something less than an animal offered to appease his animal needs. This was only what Mr. Creasey himself had suggested, of course, but to hear it from *her* was unbearable. Still, I felt there was more and I needed her to finish. I could hear slow, shuffling footsteps on the stairs to the upper gallery, as if a group of men were carrying something heavy.

"I am sorry that you have been through this dear," she said to me. "But it does not have to continue for much longer. The story has a happy ending, you see."

She was smiling again, with that same look of delight that I had noticed earlier.

"Adam was not dead, you see," she announced triumphantly. "He was a prisoner of war and he's come back to me. Which means that Bertrand Creasey was never my husband, and that he lied to me about Adam's death and his final wish. So you can sit up Mrs. Evans, if you want. The men are bringing Creasey up now. It is time to set the record straight!"

"No!" I shouted, and sat bolt upright.

At the top of the stairs I could see my husband, Mr. Jones, and the other Vicars all carrying a large hessian sack on their shoulders. There were feet sticking out of the open end of the sack, and the man inside was struggling in vain to free himself.

At the same time Sergeant Haylock finished what he was doing and pulled down an enormous dust sheet. Behind it, in the same copper and gold finish of the organ pipes, were two large-as-life statues of figures that I immediately recognised from my days in Sunday school: the golden calf, and the whore of Babylon. Each had been crafted to sit atop the pipes of the organ so that the sound would pass through them, which was unusual but not unsettling. What terrified me was that both appeared to be hollow, with holes where the eyes and mouth of each would be, as if they had been created deliberately to hold, separately, two people.

The men dropped the sack onto the floor, clearly relieved to be free of the weight, and there was an exclamation of pain and anger from inside.

I looked back at the two statues, wondering as to their purpose. Presumably the first would be Mr. Creasey, but who was to be contained within the second?

It was at that moment, lost in those thoughts, that I heard Adam Haylock speak for the first time.

"Alright Creasey?" he called in a jocular tone of voice. "Bloody good to see you, old chap."

Sergeant Haylock, a mischievous look in his good eye, flipped a clasp on the side of the calf statue and it swung open. You could see that inside there was all kind of machinery and sophistication, and all of it, so it seemed, powered by the air that would be forced through the organ pipes. There were needles and blades and cogs with flat, blunt sides. Such an array of unpleasant looking devices were there that it was impossible to distinguish what each one did. To my increasing dismay and revulsion, it was also clear that there was the space for a man inside the calf, his face pushed into the head and the rest of his body into the broad corpus of the statue.

The men, all seven Vicars, extracted Mr. Creasey from the sack and, with some effort, fastened him into the interior of the statue. Once his ample frame had been secured the devices of evident torture that were present became more comprehensible. There were many, although one, around the loins, particularly caught the eye. I cannot, to this day, understand why I did not pass out there and then.

Once Mr. Creasey was fully inside, the external shell of the statue was swung shut. The mouthpiece of the calf was closed unceremoniously and all that could be seen of

Mr. Creasey were his terrified, defiant eyes.

Next, Sergeant Haylock opened the clasp of the whore statue and stood back. I think I moaned audibly at what I saw inside, to the amusement of those present, and moaned again when he fixed me with that one, bright eye and said:

"Before we get to Creasey, I think we'll start with you, Mrs. Evans."

I looked around for William and caught my last glimpse of him descending the stairs to the nave below.

"It's no good looking to your husband," the Sergeant said. "In fact, this particular remodelling of the organ was at his request. I will be visiting all of the churches in this diocese in time, but we can consider this the prototype, if you like."

I heard Reverend Jones let out a high-pitched, boyish giggle. Nobody paid him any mind, however, as they were as transfixed as I was. I was only dimly aware of the sound.

Speechless, I looked again at the internal workings of the statue. Although there were, as with the calf into which Mr. Creasey had been interned, many sharp and unpleasant items there were also mechanics that were, quite obviously, of a sexual nature. In the seat of the statue was a large phallus, ten to twelve inches in length, which could be inserted into the crotch of the statue and, indeed, its occupant. The breast cups contained fasteners and small, delicate machinery, the purpose of which was not clear. The statue itself was arranged so that the arms and the legs were splayed wide apart, and there were also small wires that seemed designed for distributing electrical currents through many different parts of the interior, and through whoever was captive inside. Again, all of this seemed to be controlled and powered by whichever pipes were employed by the organist below.

"I have written many pieces of music, Mrs. Evans," Sergeant Haylock explained. "Some of them will bring pain, and some will bring intense pleasure. Some will combine the two. Your body will become the direct recipient of my art and your husband's skill. My wife and I, for she is still my wife, will enjoy each mass from this gallery, Mrs. Evans. The choice of music, however, will be entirely your husband's choice.

"What do you say, Mrs. Evans?"

You might expect me to have been defiant. You might have expected some sense of outrage, or moral courage at this point. None were forthcoming — Mr. Creasey had done his job too well.

"Thank you, Lord Haylock, sir," I said, and curtseyed. This was greeted by spontaneous applause from the Vicars, until Sergeant Haylock held up his hand for silence.

"Quite right, Mrs. Evans," he said. "We expected that it would be more difficult to wean you off your particular dependencies than it would be to use them to our own advantage: the creation of art, and of a good wife."

I lowered my head, ashamed.

"Now you, Creasey," Sergeant Haylock said, turning to the frightened, crying eyes that were visible inside the calf statue. "We've got a particular melody for you, and one that ends in quite a crescendo. I understand, having spoken to the Vicars, that there is need of a castrato for the choir, and I seem to remember you had a beautiful voice when we were younger."

There was laughter all around, and Mr. Creasey's eyes bulged inside the statue.

With that William, seated beside the nave below, began to play an unfamiliar tune, and the splendour of the melody all but drowned out the sounds coming from Mr. Creasey inside the golden statue.

"Bravo," applauded Mr. Jones. "Bravo!"